"What? You said you're going to sit for me tonight, right? You might have to get in there and do some extreme cleaning. By the way, why did nature give girls so many cracks and crevices? Seems a little unhygienic to me. I had to give her three butt baths in the sink yesterday." It's a full-time job keeping her clean.

"You're actually making me feel skeeved out about my own body right now."

"You? I doubt there's a place on your body I wouldn't kiss or lick." *What the hell am I saying?* I can't be flirting with her.

"Nice segue into a suck-up there, Dean. Yes. I can sit for you."

"Thank you. I appreciate it."

"Which other nights will you need me?" she asks.

I give it some thought.

OTHER WORKS BY MIMI JEAN PAMFILOFF

COMING SOON!
Wall Men (Wall Men #1) ← Horror romance.
BOO!
Never King's (King Series #8) ← Heads
will explode.
Just Mr. Love (RevoLUVtion #2) ← Will Huff
be forgiven?
The Immortal Tailor (Immortal Tailor #1) ← More
Cimil anyone?
She's Got the Time (M.O. Mack,
Suite #45 Series) ← Trouble is brewing.

THE ACCIDENTALLY YOURS SERIES
(Paranormal Romance/Humor)
Accidentally in Love with…a God? (Book 1)
Accidentally Married to…a Vampire? (Book 2)
Sun God Seeks…Surrogate? (Book 3)
Accidentally…Evil? (Novella, Book 3.5)
Vampires Need Not…Apply? (Book 4)
Accidentally…Cimil? (Novella, Book 4.5)
Accidentally…Over? (Finale, Book 5)

THE BOYFRIEND COLLECTOR DUET
(New Adult/Suspense)
The Boyfriend Collector, Part 1
The Boyfriend Collector, Part 2

FANGED LOVE
(Standalone/Paranormal/Humor)

THE FATE BOOK DUET
(New Adult/Humor)
Fate Book
Fate Book Two

THE FUGLY DUET
(Contemporary Romance)
fugly
it's a fugly life

THE HAPPY PANTS SERIES
(Standalones/Romantic Comedy)
The Happy Pants Café (Prequel)
Tailored for Trouble (Book 1)
Leather Pants (Book 2)
Skinny Pants (Book 3)

IMMORTAL MATCHMAKERS, INC., SERIES
(Standalones/Paranormal/Humor)
The Immortal Matchmakers (Book 1)
Tommaso (Book 2)
God of Wine (Book 3)
The Goddess of Forgetfulness (Book 4)
Colel (Book 5)
Brutus (Book 6)
God of Temptation (Finale)

THE KING SERIES
(Dark Fantasy/Suspense)
King's (Book 1)
King for a Day (Book 2)
King of Me (Book 3)

Mack (Book 4)
Ten Club (Book 5)
The Dead King (Book 6)
Lord King (Book 7)
Never King's (Finale) ← Coming late 2022.

THE LIBRARIAN'S VAMPIRE ASSISTANT
(Standalones/Mystery/Humor)
The Librarian's Vampire Assistant (Book 1)
The Librarian's Vampire Assistant (Book 2)
The Librarian's Vampire Assistant (Book 3)
The Librarian's Vampire Assistant (Book 4)
The Librarian's Vampire Assistant (Book 5)
Vampire Man (Book 6, Finale)

THE MERMEN TRILOGY
(Dark Fantasy/Suspense)
Mermen (Part 1)
MerMadmen (Part 2)
MerCiless (Part 3)

MR. ROOK'S ISLAND TRILOGY
(Contemporary/Suspense)
Mr. Rook (Part 1)
Pawn (Part 2)
Check (Part 3)

THE OHELLNO SERIES
(Standalones/New Adult/Romantic Comedy)
Smart Tass (Book 1)
Oh Henry (Book 2)
Digging A Hole (Book 3)

Battle of the Bulge (Book 4)
My Pen is Huge (Book 5)
Wine Hard, Baby (Book 6)
Baby, Please (Book 7) ← You are here!

REVOLUVTION SERIES
(Romance/Action/Dark Humor)
Mr. Ultra Mega Love (Book 1)
Just Mr. Love (Book 2) ← Coming soon in 2022.

SUITE #45 SERIES by M.O. MACK
(Thriller/Suspense/Action)
She's Got the Guns (Book 1)
She's Got the Money (Book 2)
She's Got the Time (Book 3) ← Coming soon in 2022.

WISH, a Standalone Novel
(Romantic Comedy)

BABY, PLEASE

The OHellNo Series
Book 7

Mimi Jean Pamfiloff

A Mimi Boutique Novel

Copyright © 2022 by Mimi Jean Pamfiloff
Print Edition

All rights reserved. No part of this publication may be reproduced, distributed, or transmitted in any form or by any means, including photocopying, recording, or other electronic or mechanical methods, without the prior written permission of the writer, except in the case of brief quotations embodied in critical reviews and certain other noncommercial uses permitted by copyright law.

This is a work of fiction. Names, characters, places, brands, media, and incidents are either the product of the author's imagination or are used fictitiously. The author acknowledges the trademarked status and trademark owners of various products referenced in this work of fiction, which have been used without permission. The publication/use of these trademarks are not authorized, associated with, or sponsored by the trademark owners.

Cover Design: Earthly Charms & Sweet 'N Spicy Designs
Developmental Editing: Stephanie Elliot
Copyediting and Proof Reading: Pauline Nolet & JRT Editing
Formatting: Paul Salvette

BABY, PLEASE

CHAPTER ONE
DEAN

What am I going to do? I slouch over the bar, my hands tightly gripping my third pint of cheap beer. *I fucked up.* I know it, my team knows it, and everyone watching the game knows it.

Today was supposed to be my big chance to show the whole damned world what I can do. Instead, they witnessed the "hottest college wide receiver to come along in a decade" crack under pressure.

The TV cameras and cheering fans got to my head. Even after Coach warned me!

Why, Dean? What the fuck? You've caught the damned ball thousands of times. And the one time it counts, you miss?

In reality, I missed five times. Every pass thrown my way. But the humiliation du jour was the final play.

There were five seconds on the clock. I was wide open on the third yard line when our quarterback threw a pass with a slow easy arc, the ball mocking the other team for allowing me to sail through their defenses unnoticed. I ran to catch the ball, the point of interception two feet inside the touchdown zone. I raised my hands to snatch our easy victory from the air.

And then I looked away.

For one split second.

And I missed.

A kindergartner could have caught it! That touchdown would have won us the game. It would have changed my life—the team's lives. My little brother's life.

Now how am I going to take care of him? Where the hell do I go from here? I'm the guy who's fought for every opportunity. The guy who came from shit—shit school, shit neighborhood, shit family— the worst this world has to offer. And after all the late nights studying (because I suck at school) and all the overtime at practice (because I was never the best player, just the hardest working), I managed a miracle: to get a shot at a better life. Full scholar- ship, too.

No, I didn't go Ivy, but O State offered a full ride, and it's only a few hours' drive to Flip, my little brother, who's currently in rehab. Again.

He's a total fuckup with a heart of gold, which is why I refuse to give up on him like everyone else has.

But make no mistake, I had my pick of colleges, and that small taste of success had me shoving my head so far up my ass that it was a miracle I could still breathe.

And then there was the infamous seven-minute segment on ESPN two weeks ago that put me on the map. How they dug up so much private information, including Flip's trouble with drugs and the law, I don't know, but they made me out to be a saint. *"The brother who made it against all odds. With the face of a GQ model."* After that, I went viral. I'm talking fan clubs—mostly women—and every major sports agency trying to sign me. *I had it all right in my hands!*

With a groan, I hang my head. *I'm a grade A asshole.*

"Hey there," says a soft voice. "You look like you're having a rough night."

I lift my head to find a blonde in a red dress who's taken the barstool next to me. She's a little older, maybe in her mid-thirties, and she's easily the prettiest woman in this shit-kicker Texas bar despite her puffy eyes. I can tell she's been crying. I'd be right there with her if I didn't consider crying a mortal sin. Where I come from, you cry, you get your ass kicked. They'll give you a reason to pray for death, too. Some rough shit.

"Yeah, very rough," I reply glumly.

"Me too." She pauses for a long, long while. I almost forget she's there. "My husband just told me he wants a divorce. *Her* name is Brittney. She's only twenty."

I grab my beer, chug half, and set it on the counter. "It's the rule. Husbands only leave their wives for younger women with peppy names ending in vowel sounds. Chrissy, Jenny, Katie."

She chuckles, and two dimples pucker at the sides of her mouth. "So how do you explain Megan, Crystal, or Michelle? Those names could belong to husband thieves."

"Ah." I take another gulp of beer, the cold bubbles tingling down my throat. "Well, the answer is simple: those names are the exception. But we all know the classic husband-robbers, the ones to really be afraid of, are the *E*s and *I*s. Stacy, Tracy, and—"

"Brittney." She bobs her head at the counter, a hint of a smile on her red lips.

I like her smile. It holds a certain maturity or wisdom, like she isn't shocked by the cruelty of life despite being wounded by it.

She's definitely older than me. Not that I care. She seems like just the distraction I need tonight.

"So what are you drinking?" I ask. "No. Wait. Let me guess." I look her over, forcing myself not to stare too long at her ample cleavage. She has nice, high breasts. Probably real. Definitely no kids.

Guys like me know that kind of stuff. Not because we are sexist pigs, which I can be, but because growing up in a rough neighborhood, you learn to size up a person quickly—how they're dressed, the color of the whites in their eyes, their posture, weapons in their pockets. Paying attention meant the difference between getting robbed and shot or making it home to a little brother who had no one, after a late practice when the buses stop running and I had to walk home.

"Go on. What's my drink of choice?" she asks.

Her hair is smooth and shiny and cut in a perfectly layered bob. Not Cheapy Cuts. Her nails are manicured and painted in a buff tone. Classy, not trashy. Her red dress is sexy and tailored, made from expensive-looking fabric instead of that stretchy stuff.

She's got money. Or, at least, her cheating husband does.

"Your drink is…French Viognier. Rhone Valley. Aged at least two years in oak." Back in Oregon, I work as a server at a wine bar during the off-season. The owner originally hired me to stock the bar and help out in the back room—needed someone who could carefully lift heavy crates. I'm a big guy at six two and weighing one-ninety-five. After a week, the owner noticed all the rich wives eyeing me during their girly brunches. He gave me a book about wine, told me to learn the basics—red, white, rose, champagne—the countries, regions, and wineries they carried. Honestly, compared to the shit I've been through, learning about fancy grape juice was a cake walk. Grape walk?

I wait for her reaction, and I'm not disappointed.

Her green eyes twinkle, and she roars with

laughter, smacking a knee. "You are full of surprises." She points a manicured finger at me and tilts her head to one side. "And not bad looking either, if you don't mind me saying."

I don't. I'm so down on myself after today's fuckup that her compliment feels like a life raft. Maybe I'm not a complete waste of clean air, even if it's only for my looks. My mom's family was Greek, so I tan pretty nicely, but it's my light hazel eyes that get the ladies' attention. In second place is my body.

That's it. My body. I never saw myself as a piece of meat, but maybe I can be one of those romance cover models since football just became a dead end. The university will let me play out my contract and finish my degree in liberal arts, but my dream of going pro is over.

Haters are already draggin' my ass all over Twitter: *"My two-year-old catches better than this hyped-up piece of crap. Nothing fresh or new about him!"* *"I've seen drunk sailors who catch better. And let's keep it real, people. Catching the clap is pretty fucking easy."*

Brutal.

"So," she says, "I told you my sad story. What's yours?"

I go into defense mode. Kind of instinctual at this point in my life. Being cautious has kept me alive.

"My girlfriend dumped me," I lie. "Has dreams of someone better." Girlfriend is code for football, in case anyone is wondering.

"Don't tell me you're one of these idiots who also went for a younger woman? You look too smart for that. And you strike me as one of those guys who likes things a certain way—disciplined in body, mind, and business."

How old does she think I am? I'm a twenty-one-year-old mess. Soaked in beer. About ready to give up on life. Still, I'd never go younger. I like women, not girls fresh out of high school.

"My ex is actually older than me," I say, wondering exactly how old football is. "And yes, I'm all about discipline."

"How refreshing. What else are you into?" she asks.

"My career. Money. Not much room for anything else."

"Wow. A finance guy."

That came out wrong. I didn't mean to make it sound like my career is money.

I let it slide. This is just a casual conversation in a bar. Not like I'm ever going to see her again.

"So what's your name?" she asks, doing a sexy little hair flip.

"I'm Dean." I hold out my hand.

"Marli." She slowly slides her hand into mine, letting our palms rub together before she administers a pulsating squeeze.

No one shakes hands like that unless they want to send a message. She wants to fuck me.

"Marli." I roll her name over my tongue and offer a devilish smile. "What a shame."

"What?"

"Now I can't take you back to my room."

"Why?" She laughs.

"Obviously, my wife will object when you steal me away."

Her smile drops, and her eyes focus on my ring-less finger. "You're married?"

"No, but I could be someday, and you'll hunt me down, begging for more."

"Will I now?" she replies, sounding intrigued. "And why would I do that?"

I lean in close and whisper, "Because after I fuck you with my giant dick, you won't ever be able to forget me."

She grins and licks her lips. "I'll take my chances."

CHAPTER TWO

Eleven months later

I'm replacing a broken fence post high on the hill along the southern property line of the Grape Ranch, a winery known for its peppery pinots just off the Oregon coast, where I've been interning all summer. My old boss from the wine bar hooked me up since he's good friends with the winery's owner, Hector. Lucky me, because after my fiasco last fall, I was forced to pick myself up by the big-boy curlies and put together a plan F.

F is for fucked.

Let's face it, though, I was never going to play football forever, and that degree in liberal arts wasn't going to cut it in the real world. So I switched majors—business with a minor in viticulture. I figured it made sense given all the winery jobs around here. And if that dries up, I'll have a business degree.

Look at me adulting.

Only now I've got a serious problem: six classes

for the fall semester. All starting next week.

I figured I would have more time to study since I anticipated being benched for the season. Life doesn't give passes to arrogant fuckers unless they deliver. *Give 'em a championship trophy, the world will forgive just about anything.* But act like a cocky asshole and then fuck it all up? You're dead to them. Which is precisely why I loaded up on classes.

Unfortunately, switching majors means I've got two and a half years of classes to take when I'm already a senior, and my full scholarship runs out after this school year. That leaves me another year and a half of college to pay for on my own. I plan to apply for financial aid, but that won't give me money to help Flip. For that, I'll need a full-time job. And then some.

I'm willing to do whatever it takes to make things happen, but then two days ago, life took another turn when Coach pulled me aside after practice.

"Everybody's behind you, Dean," he said.

When I asked what he meant, he told me everyone knows how hard it's been dealing with my brother. "But let's face facts," he added, "the scouts want to see your head in the game no matter what's going on in your personal life. Don't fuck up again."

So, basically, the football world believes last year's fuckup, the one that cost us big, was because of family issues. I get another chance, but that's it.

Just one.

I remove my baseball cap and run a hand through my sweaty hair before getting back to my fence. I clip the last wire and inspect my work. *A damned good repair job.*

I really enjoy this kind of stuff, too. No noise. No cameras. Nothing complicated to remember. It's just me, the fresh air, and lots of grapevines that don't say much. It's peaceful out here, for sure.

I step back and stare out at the long stretch of deep blue ocean off in the distance and watch the fog roll in. Soon the sky will go dark, and the air will turn drizzly and cold. Reminds me of how fucked I am.

Here's the thing: If I play well this season and pick up a pro contract, I'll have enough money to really help Flip. I would be able to afford a real therapist and private rehab for him instead of the shit, underfunded state facility he's at that only makes him worse. They've introduced him to people who keep telling him he's a victim of society and not to feel bad for being an addict, instead of giving him tough love. Bottom line, the past isn't an excuse to keep using, robbing, and being a general fuckup. He has a future, just like everyone else, and it's what a person makes of it that defines them.

I chuckle bitterly at myself and slide off my work gloves. *Listen to me. There I go with my fucking PSAs.* I'm preaching BS, like a guy who actually knows what the hell he's doing, when I should be working on my game plan.

How am I going to play this season like I mean it, which requires me to practice five times harder than anyone else, while carrying six classes? Then there's this paid internship here at the winery. It's part of the viticulture program. A big part.

I could drop all my classes and take some basket-weaving shit—see where things go this season—but if football doesn't pan out (and there's a good chance it won't), I'll be exactly where I started: with a pile of classes to take, short on funds to graduate, and having to borrow even more money, all the while Flip rots away in that place.

Worse yet, they'll eventually let him out when he doesn't have his shit together, so he'll just end up robbing some poor person again. Of course, he'll get caught. He always does. And next time, he might land in prison, not rehab.

Point is, the clock is ticking on any possibility of a future for him if I don't get him some real help. I have to take this shot at football and not fuck up this time. But I also can't afford to ease up on classes and add even more time to my graduation.

Hector, the owner of the Grape Ranch, already told me he can hook me up with a job after I graduate. He hinted at fifty grand a year to start, plus benefits. It's a job I'll need if I'm not drafted to the NFL.

Part of me prays I'm not. The pressure is insane. The other part of me wants to prove myself to the world.

I stand silent, watching the fog roll in and obscure the low-lying hills below. Row after row of lush green grapevines disappear under a blanket of pure white. For one brief moment, the horizon line above the fog turns into an amazing display of sherbet oranges and fiery reds as the sun sets.

Incredible.

I really love working here at the vineyard—being outdoors, using my hands, feeling part of something that doesn't require an audience. I don't know if I want to play ball anymore, but I have to try to go pro. For Flip and me. Millions of dollars is life-changing money.

That's right, Dean, only an idiot would turn away from a second chance at a dream life.

"Dean, what do you mean you're dropping classes to play this season?" says Nina, my neighbor who lives downstairs in our fifty-apartment complex. I've known her for about a year, ever since I moved into my three-bedroom place with a couple of teammates, Mike and Igor. Both play defense. Igor doesn't speak much English—he's a student from Ukraine—and Mike comes from the Rust Belt. He hates Oregon with a passion, but he got a full ride like me.

I plop down on Nina's blue plaid couch, and

she hands me a cold beer from her fridge.

"Thanks." I ignore her comment about school, pick up the remote on her coffee table, and switch the channel from that nasty Lifetime to ESPN.

"Dean, I'm talking to you." She snatches away the remote and turns off the TV.

"Hey. I wanted to watch that."

She rolls her eyes and sits next to me. "You always do this when you're stressed out."

Huh? We barely know each other, even though we hooked up after I first moved in. Mike and Igor were having a party, and she showed up. It happened. The next day we both decided it was a mistake. Better off as friends. Also, she'd just gotten in a fight with her manwhore boyfriend, and while they'd technically been broken up, she wasn't over him. They got back together the next week. Then they broke up again. 'Cause he was fucking his way through her friend list.

Like I said, manwhore.

Now Nina and I hang out every once in a while. She's dragged me to a couple of family functions as her date to keep her parents from ragging on her about being single. In exchange, I get a friend who's completely removed from the whole football thing. A plus when you're questioning the sanity of the people around you who eat, sleep, and breathe football. She gets how hard it is since she's on the university's track team, and her circle of friends is like a cult, too.

"Dean, what's going on?" She folds her arms across her chest. She's kind of flat. Mostly because she's a runner. No body fat. Add in her short brown hair and you've got the complete tomboy look. I'm cool with it, though I do prefer women with more curves.

Also, too often, Nina and I dress alike. I'm all about jeans—like today—and sweatshirts. Hoodies are great too since it's always drizzling around here.

"What?" I ask.

"You only come down to my apartment when you've got shit to unload. So unload."

"Not this time. I just want to watch TV on a real screen, and Mike's hogging ours." He's on some war movie kick. Says it helps him get ready for the season. Killing. Battle. *Really?*

I reach for the remote, and she slaps my hand away.

"Hey," I protest.

"Dean, I've known you for a minute, so I'm going to give you a piece of advice: You worry too much."

I frown. "That's not advice. And no I don't."

"Bullshit." She laughs. "I've never met a guy who's so wound up, he literally reminds me of a catapult. And I'm talking those medieval ones they used to launch flaming balls of exploding tar at castles."

I'm not getting the analogy. "I'm intense. Not wound up. There's a difference." I turn toward her on the couch. "And even if I were wound up, what's your point?"

"You need to start getting real about your life—make a plan that's focused and practical. Right now, you're just pushing yourself as hard as you can on every front. That's not a plan. That's just a path to a mental breakdown and imminent failure. You need to be strategic."

Stupid advice. She doesn't understand where I come from or the burden on my shoulders. My life is about plans. And backup plans. And backups to my backup plans.

"I'll get right on that," I say, "just as soon as I figure out how not to fuck up the season and throw my plan B," really my plan F, "into a shit pile, in case I fuck up the season." Which I probably will if I don't figure out how I screwed up in the first place.

Nina shakes her finger at my face. "See. That's what I'm talking about. You're trying to control everything. Plan for everything. Work for everything. Make it happen," she says, mocking my voice. "But it's not sustainable, Dean."

"Oh no?" Now I fold *my* arms across *my* chest. "Then do tell, Missy Perfect."

She narrows her eyes. "Dean, I'm being serious."

"Me too."

She takes my hand, giving it a gentle squeeze. "You have to let go of this delusion you can spin every single plate on your table. At some point you'll drop them all and end up with nothing because you're such a perfectionist—you'll kill yourself trying to 'make it happen.'"

Make it happen is my mantra, and why not? When I face impossible obstacles, like coming up with ten thousand dollars on the fly to pay for a good lawyer for Flip after he stole a car and crashed it, I made it happen. I worked overtime, moved furniture on the weekends, and I even gave private sessions at the gym. All while I took a full load of classes. Of course, it had been during the off-season, but I managed to come up with the money. Kept Flip out of jail. It was just a Band-Aid, of course, which is why I need to make this new plan happen.

"I don't see anything wrong with wanting to be the best at what I do," I say. "But let's keep it real; I'm no perfectionist. Did you see that game last fall?"

"I can't believe you're still spinning over that. One bad game. One. Poor you." She chuckles condescendingly. "But of course I saw it. I've also listened to you cry at least three times." She mocks my deep voice, "It's over for me, Nina. Over..."

That's not fair. In my defense, it was only one time, and I'd had four beers. Also, I teared up, not cried. Mostly because I still don't understand where it all went wrong. I had my plan. I executed the plan: Practice. Practice. Practice. A dash of homework and studying. More practice. Gym.

"I hear you, Nina. And I appreciate you trying

to have my back," I lower my voice and teasingly add, "because it really makes my dick hard. But I thought we both agreed we weren't going to be fuck buddies."

She stares, shooting daggers with her angry, twitching brown eyes. "You think you're so funny."

"No. My dick is really hard right now. Wanna see?" I reach for my pants.

"Stop it. I know what your dick looks like, and if it were hard right now, it would be pretty damned visible."

She means it's big. "Thank you."

"And," she adds, "I'd be pouring my ice-cold beer on it."

I stick out my lower lip. "Sure you don't want to see it anyway? Maybe pop it in your mouth?"

"You're a pig."

Sometimes. But right now, I just want Nina to drop the anti-pep talk. If I wanted to have a deep conversation about my work ethic, fucked head, or life plan, I'd be talking to Coach. Or Igor. Fine, I do talk to Nina once in a while, too, but right now, I just need to chill. Watch the game. Drink a beer.

"I'm sorry, but your comment has offended me," I say jokingly. "I'm going to have to rescind my offer. No dick viewing for you. But how about this awesome fucking game on TV?" I snatch the remote from her hand.

"Dean!"

"What?"

"You can't keep burying your head in the sand. Your tactics are going to catch up to you. I know firsthand. I had to walk away from my dreams of going to the Olympics because I wouldn't stop pushing myself to be perfect—perfect student, daughter, sister, friend, and athlete. After a while, I stopped sleeping, eating, enjoying life, because I was killing myself to be everything to everyone instead of focusing on me—my future, my dreams, and my goal."

I sigh. My dick jokes didn't work. She's not going to let this go.

I stand to leave. "Thanks for the beer."

"Where are you going?" She stands, too.

"Look, Nina, I know you care, but what do you want me to say?" I finally lose my patience. "I *was* living my dream. I was happy. I had everything figured out. And look what happened." I blew it.

"Because you told yourself everything had to be so perfect that you crumbled under the pressure. You felt trapped."

"How the fuck do you know what I felt?"

"Because when you talk, I listen."

Oh. "Well, thank you for that."

She reaches for my hand again. "I care about you, Dean. More than you know."

I suddenly realize she's looking at me a certain way. The way a woman looks at you when she has feelings. Relationship-type feelings.

I thought we agreed to just be friends.

I pull my hand away. A girlfriend is not a plate I can spin right now. "Nina, I really don't want to go there—"

"I can tell you're about to say something stupid, so just don't." She walks over to her front door and opens it. "I haven't asked you for anything because I don't expect anything. But right now, I need you to go."

"Thanks. You've been a good friend." A hot friend, too. Maybe that's part of the reason I like talking to her. She's nice to look at. Sort of a bonus. "And you can look at my dick anytime. I mean it."

She shakes her head. "Jackass."

I kiss her on the cheek and leave.

CHAPTER THREE

I take the stairs up to my place, a tiny scratching sensation in the back of my brain. Nina's never been a pushy or preachy chick. It's why I like hanging out with her. So maybe there's a reason she thinks I'm biting off more than I can chew.

Even if she's right, which she's not, because I'm always right, what does it change? Nothing.

I can't bail on Flip. Which means I can't bail on playing football or plan F. I'm not going to make the same mistake of putting all my balls in one basket.

I reach the third floor and get to our door. The apartments here remind me of prison—everything painted in gray or khaki. The balconies and walkways are concrete and open up to unkempt gardens overgrown with weeds, or to the parking lot that encircles the complex. Not a lot of fluff, but the apartments are big. Rent is cheap.

I walk inside our beige-carpeted living room to find Mike sitting on our beat-up navy-blue couch. He's a big guy, like me, but with blond hair and a leaner body. He's known as Mr. Smiles because the girls always comment on his "cute smile." I really don't see anything special about it. Except that right now, his smile is missing, and he's leaning forward, his hands clasped together. Probably fought with his girlfriend of the week again. He goes through women like Muscle Milk.

"What's up?" I ask and go to the fridge in our shit-brown kitchen—stove, fridge, cabinets all brown—searching for a fresh beer.

"Someone's here to see you. She's waiting in your room."

Probably that girl Kari I've been texting with from a party I went to last week. I didn't stay long—wasn't in the mood to socialize—but she and I flirted for a few minutes over by the keg. I shouldn't have given her my number because she's been hitting me up every day.

But why would Mike look worried?

I suddenly hear a baby crying.

With a beer in hand, I pass through the living room on my way to my bedroom. "What's with the baby?" I ask Mike.

"It's yours."

"Funny." These guys are always playing practical jokes. "I just met Kari, so not likely."

"I don't know who the fuck Kari is, but there's definitely a baby in your room."

I stop in my tracks. He's fucking with me. Must be a speaker hidden in there, making all that noise.

"Asshole." I shake my head and enter my sparsely decorated room. It's the first door on the left just before the bathroom. The other two rooms are on the right side of the hallway. My room is the only one that doesn't stink like old socks, but that's because I keep everything neat—either hanging in the closet or folded in my dresser. I have a chipped-up desk and chair for studying that I got at a secondhand store, but I prefer to study at the library. Mike and Igor like to have girls over and make noise. Noise gets in the way of my tight schedule: Sleep. Work out. Work. Football practice. Study. Repeat.

And speaking of noise... What is that? A baby carrier and a plastic grocery bag are sitting on my king-size bed.

I walk over and look down at the fat little pink thing crying its eyes out.

I go back out to the living room and point to my doorway. "There's a fucking baby in my room, Mike."

"Yeah, dipshit. I know." Mike's eyes zero in on a thick manilla envelope sitting on our wooden coffee table. "The woman said her name was Marli. She left you that."

I blink, trying to get a fucking grip on what's happening. My roommates can be major dicks when it comes to pranks, but that's a real fucking baby in there. Seems like an extreme prop.

I go for the envelope and unfold the handwritten letter that's thicker than a Bible.

Dear Dean,

It took a while to track you down through the hotel we stayed at back in Houston; otherwise, I would've contacted you sooner. Oh, hell. Maybe I wouldn't have. Who knows? All I can say is that I've spent the last eleven months trying to make sense of my life after my husband left. By the time I figured out I was pregnant, something I was told by doctors to be impossible after years of fertility treatments, I didn't know what to do.

I've always wanted a baby. But that was when I had a husband, a house, and dreams of a future. After John left, I wasn't sure if I was at a place in my life to be a single mother. That's part of the reason I didn't try to find you. What would be the point if I wasn't sure I'd keep the baby? Your baby.

Then the weeks dragged on, and John called out of the blue. He and Brittney broke up. He wanted to reconcile. I said no. I meant it, too. But then slowly we began talking on the phone. A conversation here and there.

Long story short, Dean, this was the other reason I didn't contact you. I started to think that maybe John and I could work it out. But I knew if he found out about me being pregnant, he might not want me back. He's always been the jealous type.

Anyway, we talked on the phone for

months, and he's been begging to see me, but I needed to make him wait until after the baby was born. I planned to give her up for adoption and tell John about it all later. Much later. Maybe never.

But then she came, Dean. I took one look at Fia and knew I could never give her up.

So now, I'm asking you to take her, just for a week. I have very little money, and I can't leave her with anyone I know—not family, not friends. Word would get back to John before our big reunion. I need time to tell him about her. I know you are a good guy with great potential, Dean, even if you lied about being in finance. Yes, I've done my research on you.

I've left instructions on how to feed Fia, her nap schedule, and other important tips. You'll have to buy formula and diapers in a few days because I couldn't afford to get more. In the bag is a book, kind of a baby manual. Be sure to support her neck when you carry her.

See you in a week.

Marli

Still gripping the letter, I drop my hand. *Ohellno! This has to be a fucking joke.* But that baby wailing in the other room isn't. She has a pair of lungs like a seal or dolphin, or whichever mammal has huge lung capacity.

The shrill of her cries pierces my ears.

"This can't be happening!" Panicked, I thumb through the sheets of paper. Marli left a phone number for emergencies.

I pull out my cell from my jeans pocket and dial, but it goes straight into voicemail.

"Marli, it's Dean. You have to call me right away." I give my number and hang up.

"Dude, you gotta do something about that baby." Mike presses his hands over his ears.

"Do what? I don't know shit about babies."

"Then call the cops or something. They'll know what to do."

I give Mike's suggestion a quick thought. "I can't do that. They'll put the baby with Child Services."

"What other choice do you have? You can't take care of it."

"Maybe Marli will come back?" I say.

"And if she doesn't? Or worse, what if she does? That woman was a total dumpster fire—rambling incoherently, bawling, hiccupping. Which means that baby has to go to Child Services eventually." He pauses. "Unless you plan to keep her forever?"

No. No way. I can't even keep her for a day. I have work in the morning, and I need the money. I don't get a lot for living expenses, so every penny counts. Luckily, classes don't start until next week, but evening practices have been in full swing for a month because our first game is next Sunday, a week from now. The only reason we have today off is because Coach wanted us to rest up. Bottom line, though, there is no room in my schedule for a baby.

"You have to call the police," Mike pushes. "That woman just left her kid here. Messed up, man."

"I know, but…" My stomach squeezes into a tight knot.

"But what? Is the baby really yours?"

I shrug. "How the hell should I know?"

"Did you bag it?" Mike looks at my groin.

I honestly don't remember if I used a condom. "I was fucked up. Had too much from the minibar."

"Dude! Seriously? What's the number one rule? You wrap that shit up. Not unless you want hordes of little Deanies running around, asking for a cut of your paycheck until they're eighteen."

"I'm always careful." At least, I try to be. Condoms have been known to bust on me. Big-dick problems. "But I met Marli *that* night. You know. Eleven months ago?"

Mike gives me a knowing look. "Oh. *That* night."

Yes, the night my life seemed over. The great flop. Dean "the Mighty" Norland became Dean No-Land. Because I couldn't land one touchdown, even when it was handed to me on a silver platter.

"So the screaming banshee in your room could actually be yours?" Mike asks.

I exhale with a groan and run both hands through my hair. "Yeah. I guess so."

"Welp, not sure that changes much. You still gotta call, man. You can't take care of it, and what sort of mom just leaves her kid with a stranger?"

I agree with everything Mike is saying, especially the part about leaving a baby with a person you don't know. Who the hell does that?

A crazy person, that's who.

Proof being how Marli says she did it so she could get back together with her cheating husband, who may or may not want her if he finds out she has a baby.

That's one fucked-up situation.

What's even more fucked up is dumping off your child with a twenty-two-year-old guy you don't even know. It's the kind of thing my own mom would've done, although most of the time she forgot we existed and left us alone for days.

Eventually, those days turned into a week. Then another. The school found out we weren't being looked after, so we were put with Child Services until they got a hold of my uncle Norm. They placed us with him temporarily at first, but temporarily turned to permanent after my mother just plain disappeared.

Meanwhile, Norm had his own issues with life. Drugs. Alcohol. Whatever. We barely saw him since he was a musician and traveled to gigs ninety-nine percent of the time. Every few weeks he'd show up, pay rent or buy us groceries, and give us what little money he could spare. That was about it.

So Flip and I were left on our own. Me, ten years old, taking care of a six-year-old. Pretty messed up. When I became a teen, I got into trouble a lot—going to school drunk, high, or not at all. That's when the principal caught me with weed and gave me a choice: get my shit together and join the football team or go to juvie. I couldn't leave Flip alone, so I took the deal.

But while I got straight, Flip got worse. Wilder. Angrier. By the time I graduated high school, he'd been to juvie twice. Norm always got him out and tried to help Flip with "stern talks," but the truth was, Flip needed a parent, and parents we were not.

Eventually, Norm gave up. We fought about it and stopped talking. Now I'm all Flip's got.

"I can't call the cops," I say to Mike, with a dread-filled sigh. "Not yet."

"Why?"

"Because if I do, that baby's going into the system, and she might never get out." And a half-bad mother is better than none at all or going into foster care. Marli is the lesser of evils.

Mike stares at me like he doesn't get it. How could he? He grew up in a small town with a big family and food on the table. He went to church every Sunday and celebrated Christmas with presents under the tree.

"It's just one week," I add. "If Marli doesn't return, I'll make the call."

"Dude, you're insane. Who's going to watch the

baby while you're at work? Or practice?"

I give it some thought. "Nina can help. And maybe I can find a daycare for a few hours." I have a couple hundred bucks in my account. "I'll figure it out. I'll make it happen."

Mike rolls his eyes. "Well, can you make it stop crying?"

I freeze in place. "What if she needs her diaper changed?"

Mike gets up, leaves the room, and shuts his bedroom door.

"What a friend." I slide my phone from my pocket and search the internet on how to change a baby.

I find a video and tap play. "Jesus! It's like a crime scene. Made of poop!" I tilt my head to the side, wondering how the hell you get all those crevices clean. *Wipe front to back. Okay, but…gross, man! Just gross.*

I go into my bedroom and look down at the red-faced infant, who reminds me of a demon, flailing its fat little arms, hiccupping like mad, eyes clenched tight. I'm pretty sure she's about to explode if I don't do something.

I reach down and pat the bundle of rage on her fat little leg. "Hello, angry little person. I'm Dean, your d-d-nanny. I'm your *nanny*. Well, not really because I don't know how to take care of you. But if you stop crying, I'll stop freaking the fuck out." My heart is racing a million miles a second. I don't know the first thing about babies. What if I do something wrong and break it?

She continues yelling, and I have no choice but to just get in there and *ass*-ess the situation.

I lean down and carefully unlatch her from the car seat, avoiding touching her. "Okay. Step one is done. See. I got this." I slap my hands together and rub my palms, warming them up for the next big step. "Here goes." I go in for the tiny howling demonic creature, gently lifting her from the seat. I support her tiny head like Marli's letter said.

Oh wow. I give her a little bounce in my hands. *She's lighter than a football. So tiny.* I've never held a baby, but I must be doing something right because Fia immediately stops crying. But now I'm the one screaming. Something squishy, warm, and wet smudged on my arm. And the smell. Nasty!

"Don't pass out, Dean. Don't pass out." I suddenly notice the baby staring with her big gray eyes. She has the tiniest little lips and the smallest little brown eyelashes. Her nose is the size of a button. I don't see myself in any of her features other than she's damned cute.

"How could your mama leave you, little girl?" I just don't get it. But I'll do what I can to keep her safe. It's just one week. How hard could it be, right?

CHAPTER FOUR

"*Choo* out of your mind, Dean," says Igor, emerging from his room at three in the morning. "She no stay here. Igor needs sleep."

Igor's nickname is the Yellow Squash. Mostly because his hair is light blond, and he loves to squash things. Luckily for him, though, his body is shaped like the Hulk.

I continue pacing across the beige carpet of our living room with the hysterical, crying baby in my arms. "I don't know what's wrong. I gave her a bottle, just like the instructions said. I changed her and almost died doing it. Now she won't sleep— and I've tried rocking her, singing, and—"

Igor walks over and holds out his arms. "Baby, please."

"Thanks, man. I need a few hours of sleep before work." I hand Fia over.

"I no take. I show you *seester's* way, like she do with my niece." Igor takes Fia and gently presses her to his shoulder. He gives her a few pats, and suddenly she burps. A glob of white stuff dribbles from her mouth onto his shirt.

Yikes. "Are babies supposed to leak milk like that?"

Igor hands her back. "No leak. You *forgeet* to burp her. And you owe me new *sheert*." He disappears into his room.

I look down at a sleepy-eyed little Fia, who seems just fine now. *And I thought grown women were difficult.* "You're lucky you're so cute."

I take her to my room and tuck her into her car seat. Marli left a small portable bassinet, but I couldn't figure out how to put it together. There were no instructions.

I'll deal with it in the morning. I plop facedown on my bed and feel my mind crashing from exhaustion. *Morning?*

My eyes fly open. Shit. I have to be at work in three hours, and I didn't find someone to watch Fia. I'd been too wrapped up in reading all the instructions Marli wrote out. Of course, half the things didn't make sense, so I had to look up a bunch of stuff on the internet or in the baby book. I thought I had it all figured out—feed baby, put baby down to sleep, keep baby clean. Piece of cake! Until baby started to cry for no damned reason.

Except that I forgot to burp her.

I roll over onto my back and stare at the ceiling. I'm going to have to call in sick and come up with a plan for the week.

I'll ask Nina to help, of course. Maybe she has

some friends who have babysitting experience.

Wait. A thought hits me. I can't go around telling everyone this is my kid. (A) I don't actually know that she is. (B) Either way, I'm not keeping Fia. Marli will either return, or I'll hand Fia to Child Services. Either way, I'll have to explain to my friends where she came from.

I need to come up with a story.

"Oh no. You're sick?" says Lara, the admin at the Grape Ranch, over the phone.

"Yeah, can you give Hector the message?" I cough for effect. "I have a real bad headache."

"Hopefully it's nothing serious."

"No," I say, "it's not. But let the boss man know I'll look at my schedule and see if I can make up the missed day later this week." Hector has been working hard, getting the vineyard into shape after the harvest. I keep wondering if he might be planning to sell it, considering all the upgrades and cleanup he's been doing. Kind of worries me because I might need that job after graduation. On the other hand, Hector is a really different kind of guy—used to be a monk—and he believes in taking care of people. If he did sell, I know he'd make his employees part of the deal.

Worry about it later, Dean. Right now, I need to have a plan for Fia. Thank God classes don't start until next week.

"Will do," says Lara. "Call if you need anything. Like soup or some company or—"

"No. I'm great. Thanks. Just going to sleep it off."

"All right." She sounds a little disappointed by my answer, but I don't have time to care.

I say goodbye and decide it's time to head downstairs and introduce Fia to Nina before she leaves for work. She's been teaching Zumba in the late mornings just until the semester starts back up. Hopefully, Nina can help me out this evening when I go to practice.

I wrap Fia in her tiny pink blanket and march down to Nina's, where the music is blasting. After I knock ten times, the music stops, and she answers the door.

"Ohmygod. Who is this?" Nina's brown eyes go wide the moment she spots the adorable bundle of chubbiness in my arms.

"This is Fia, my niece."

Nina frowns. "Your brother has a baby?"

"No, my sister does. She lives in, uh, Texas."

"How come you never mentioned her?"

Because I made her up. "She's older, yanno, we're not real close, but she had an emergency and asked me to take care of her for a week."

"She flew all the way out here last night?"

I admit, it sounds sketchy, but it's the best excuse I have. "Yeah, look at my eyes. I didn't get any sleep."

"I bet."

"So, um, think you can help me out and watch her tonight while I go to practice?" I offer my most charming smile. The one that shows off my dimples, even though they're probably not very visible since I've let my beard grow out a little.

"You want *me* to watch her?"

"I'd ask Mike or Igor, but obviously they'll be at practice, too." Players are only allowed time off for things like injuries, illness, or bereavement, but that's about it. They expect us to be one hundred percent committed. "Plus," I add, "you're a woman, so…"

"So what?" Nina narrows her eyes.

"So you know what to do with babies." She's the one with the baby equipment. Not me.

Nina laughs. "God, you're hilarious sometimes."

She thinks I was joking?

Nina sighs with an amused smile. "I'd love to help out, but I have a charity event tonight. Maybe later this week?"

Tonight would be better, but I'll take what I can get. "Cool. Thank you, Nina."

She leans toward me, closely inspecting Fia's face. "Funny. You look a little like your uncle. Dontcha?"

Thankfully, Fia can't respond with the truth: that I might be the father. Her little eyes just seem to dart around, like she's taking in the surroundings.

She's smart.

"I don't see any family resemblance myself," I say to deflect suspicion. "I'll text you tomorrow?"

"Sure. Sounds good."

I start walking away, heading toward the stairwell.

"Just remember what I said about the plates, Dean."

"Thanks." I keep going. I know she means I should not have agreed to take care of this baby while working and going to practice. But I can handle it. Just as long as Marli comes back by Sunday night, I'll be fine. *Totally got this under control.*

CHAPTER FIVE

Around noon, I've got Fia down for a nap, and I'm about to take one, too. I've been through a lot of tough things, but the past eighteen hours take the cake.

I keep telling myself it's only a challenge like any other, my goal simple: make it through the week. Beyond that, I don't know. Honestly, Fia's just another chick I don't have time for. So other than having to acknowledge she's pretty damned cute and that I really feel bad for her—Marli should not have dumped her like that—I can't allow myself to feel anything.

It's just a babysitting job. I mean, why treat it any other way? Even if she *is* mine, which is something I'm not prepared to confront, I can't take care of her. I'm barely taking care of Flip and myself. And I'm not ready to be a father! That's a freaking eighteen-year commitment. *Jesus! What if she's one of those kids who wants to live with me forever? I'll never get my life back!*

See. That settles it. No keeping the baby, no

matter what. If Marli doesn't return, I know what I have to do. And that means I can't afford to get attached.

I'm about to close my navy-blue blackout curtains when there's a knock at the front door. Mike and Igor are out, enjoying their final days before the semester starts, so it's up to me to answer.

Fuck. I really need to rest up before practice tonight. I know Coach is going to make us run through all the plays for Sunday's game. To me, it's the most important one of the season because it sets the tone for everything else. If you kick ass in the first game, the team's energy feeds off it. If we get our asses kicked, the entire season will feel like an uphill battle. Morale will be low.

I pry myself from bed, go to the front door, and look through the peephole. It's Lara from work. I have no clue why she's here on her lunch break.

I open the door a few inches so she knows not to come in. "Hey, what's up?" I say, faking a scratchy throat.

Lara looks like her usual cute self with her blonde hair up in a ponytail. She's wearing a purple Grape Ranch cardigan and those snug khakis that show off her cute round ass. Not that I stare at it when we're at work, because that's what creepy assholes do, but it's hard not to notice the nice shape when she's walking away.

"I brought you soup, some chamomile tea, and lemon drops." She holds up a grocery bag.

"Wow. That's so nice."

"I can set you up if you want?"

Meaning, she wants to come in and play nurse.

"Naw. I'm good. Wouldn't want you to catch anything. This was really thoughtful, though." I take the bag from her hand and slide it through the narrow opening.

"What's that all over the front of your shirt?" She makes a sour face.

I look down at Fia's handiwork. Baby puke. "Oh, uh, I spilled some cream of chicken down my shirt. Had an early lunch. But I'll be sure to enjoy this soup for dinner."

"Are you sure you don't want me to make you some tea or—"

A piercing cry explodes from inside my room.

"Is that a baby?" Lara asks.

I flick my thumb over my shoulder. "TV. I have the volume too loud. I'll see you back at work—"

"Dean, that is not a TV. What's going on?"

"Nothing," I say.

"Bullshit. You're hiding something." She pushes past me, following the sound.

"Wait. This is my place. You can't just barge…" My voice trails off. It's too late. Lara's in my bedroom, pointing down at the baby.

"TV, huh?" Lara's brown eyes narrow.

"Oh. *That* baby. I can explain."

❧ ❦

"Ohmygoodness, what a pair of lungs." Lara tries to comfort a crying Fia by gently bouncing her. "I'm guessing she just has a little gas. Moving her around a little should help."

The little toot sound from her butt confirms it. The baby's butt, of course. *Would be weird if Lara was just standing around my room passing gas.*

"Wow. You really seem to know what you're doing," I say as I watch Fia settle right down like nothing happened.

"I babysat in high school a lot," she explains. "So when's your sister coming back?"

Yes, I told her the sister lie.

I shrug. "She said by Sunday."

"And she just dumped her baby on you?"

"She's my niece. I have to help."

"So why did you lie to me?" Lara arches a light brown brow.

"Technically, I didn't lie to you. I was leaving a message for Hector. And I wasn't in the mood to explain every complicated detail about my family's drama."

"*Technically*, you lied to me twice. Once on the phone and just now when you said it was the TV making that noise. Why lie? And don't use Hector as an excuse. We both know when it comes to compassion, he's a saint. There was no reason to call in sick when he would give you time off to help your family. So if you're not telling people the truth, there's a reason."

Yep, Lara is smart. And beautiful with blonde hair that sometimes looks golden in the light. Other times, the color comes off as a soft caramel. She's also older than me by a few years. Totally has her act together, too—college degree in business, a good-paying job, plans to run her own winery someday. For now, she's officially Hector's admin, but in such a small operation, that job title comes with five other hats, which is why Lara took the position. She's learning the operation. What I'm getting at is, she's too intelligent to buy my stupid story. But also, if someone can give me advice, it's her.

I clear my throat and gesture at the wiggly bundle in Lara's arms. "She's mine. I think."

Lara's face turns ghost white. "Sorry?"

"Her mother dropped her off when I wasn't home and left a note, saying she's my daughter. She asked me to take care of Fia for the week."

"Did you know about her?" Lara sits on my bed, still holding Fia just as naturally as ever. I'm impressed.

"No. I met her mom last year. I was at a bar, having a rough night, and we…you know."

"So no condom?" Lara snaps.

"I don't need your judgment."

"I'm only trying to establish that this baby *could* actually be yours."

"She's mine for the next six days. After that, who knows?"

"Okay, well." Lara stands and hands Fia over.

I cradle her in my arms, securing her like a football I don't want to drop.

She adds, "I hope it all works out for you." Lara turns to leave. She seems annoyed. Or pissed. I'm not sure why.

"You're going?"

"Yep. Gotta get back to the Ranch. And *you* need to come clean with Hector."

I don't want her to go. Not before I can ask for her help. "Wait. Why are you mad?"

"I'm not mad, Dean, I'm—well, I'm shocked. I thought you were a man, not a boy who goes around knocking up strange women in bars."

"Whoa." I follow her as she heads to the front door. "You're calling me a player? That's a little unfair."

Lara turns. "Did you not fuck some stranger you met in a bar?"

"Yes, but—"

"Did she not just dump a baby off on you? A baby she says is yours?"

"Yes, but—"

"Doesn't sound like a respectable guy who's got his shit together." Lara looks at Fia. "Sorry for the swearing, sweetie."

I push my hand against the door to stop Lara from opening it. She's not leaving until I give her a piece of my mind. "You know what? I don't get you women."

"What?" she snaps.

"If the tables were turned, and you showed up on my doorstep with a baby because you hooked up with some guy in a bar and made one bad choice, and then I treated you like a piece of shit—excuse my language, Fia—you'd call the feminist army on my ass or have me hanged for being a judgmental chauvinist."

Lara looks at me, then Fia. She knows I'm right. If she were the one with a surprise baby, she would expect me and everyone else to be supportive, not blameful.

I continue, "I know I lied, but now I'm telling you the truth because I could use some help here, and I respect your opinion."

Lara's gaze flutters shamefully to the floor. "I'm sorry, Dean," she says with a remorseful sigh. "You're absolutely right. What can I do to help?"

"I..." My voice trails off. Mostly because I'm too tired to have a tough conversation about something that's been mulling around in my head. Something I don't want to talk about but should because Lara is the perfect person to have this discussion with. She's logical, kind, and detached from this mess.

I decide to hold off confronting the topic for another time, until I have the mental bandwidth.

"You...?" Lara urges.

"Can you babysit tonight?"

She groans and throws her head back.

"I take it that's a no?" I say.

She offers a consoling smile. "I can do any night this week except tonight. It's a friend's birthday, and I'm throwing her a little get-together at my place."

Fuck. I can't miss tonight's practice. Not after Coach said he's giving me another chance to be in the starting lineup on Sunday. He needs to see I'm all in. Also, I'm contractually obligated to be there.

"No problem," I say. "But, yeah, I'll take you up on your offer. How about tomorrow night?"

"Sure," she says. "I'm here for you. Whatever you need." The warm, compassionate look in her eyes sparks instant discomfort in my chest. I don't know why, but I don't have the time to care.

"You okay?" she asks, squeezing my shoulder gently. "Because you look like you just swallowed a bee."

I frown and take a small step back. "Huh?"

"Dean, why are you suddenly acting like my kindness repels you?"

Because I feel uncomfortable right now but won't admit it 'cause I'm a guy. "Not sure what you mean. It's all good."

She shakes her head. "Whatever you say. Just know there's no judgment from me. From here on out, I've got your back." She opens the door and steps outside.

"Why?" I ask, staring at her blonde ponytail as she walks away.

She says over her shoulder, "Why not?"

"Because you don't know me." We're casual

work acquaintances. Nothing more.

"I think it's *you* who doesn't know *me*."

My entire life, I've been on my own. Never expected much from anyone. What was the point? It's always been up to me to *"make it happen."* I guess it feels foreign or wrong or weird or—I dunno—it feels off when people go out of their way to help for no reason. Don't get me wrong, people do nice things for me all the time. Especially women. But that's different. Those people always want something in return. The team wants me to play well so they look good. Women want to be my girlfriend because they only think with their vaginas. That's right. I'm just a sex object to them. Arm candy. Friends, well, I don't have many true friends, but I often find myself questioning them. What do *they* want?

With Lara, suddenly, I'm asking myself the same thing—*What does she want?*—only now, I'm asking because maybe I want to give it.

"You could be right," I call out to her. "I don't know you, but I'd like the chance to change that." *What the fuck am I doing?* I don't have room for another plate on my table.

"See you tomorrow." She waves goodbye, not bothering to turn around, before she disappears into the stairwell at the end of the hall.

I close the door, and a tickle pokes at my heart. I think I like that woman.

Yeah, but you'd be a selfish idiot if you go for her.

I'm not relationship material. Proof being, I've never been in one. And right now, what would be the point of starting something when I'm so damned busy? She'd feel ignored.

The current woman in my life starts making cooing sounds in my arms.

"What am I going to do with you, huh?" I've come up empty-handed in the sitter department.

I go back to my room and set Fia down in her car seat. I really need to figure out how to put together that portable bassinet. The thing has snaps and zippers and... *It looks like a pair of pants from the '80s.*

"I think I saw Michael Jackson wearing this in the 'Thriller' video," I tell Fia, not that she understands me.

I stand over her, hands on my waist, staring down at this tiny person. She looks out of place in my room, which has one lamp, a desk and chair, and a bed. The walls are pretty bare except for a few plaques I've earned while on the team—mostly stupid stuff, like most push-ups or biggest biceps. Coach gives them out at the end of each season at our banquet. The real trophies go to the guys who play in almost every game and bring the wins. My first two years, I was basically a bench player. I played just a little. Last year, Coach said I was ready to be in the starting lineup, and I played like a god. *Until I didn't.*

This is my fourth season, and I have to play like

a god the entire time, or I'm done. No team will draft me.

"What am I doing, Fia?" I ask her. "I should be getting my head straight, not playing daddy."

I dig my cell from my pocket and dial Marli again.

Voicemail.

"Marli, come on. You gotta call me back. You can't just abandon your baby like this. Call me."

CHAPTER SIX

By four o'clock, I feel like I'm mastering the baby care basics. Feeding Fia is the easiest. You measure with the scooper, add formula to the bottle along with warm bottled water, and give it a quick shake. Easy.

Not easy? When you try to eat and hold her at the same time, and then you look away from your turkey avocado sandwich for a moment, and she smooshes her hand in it.

Damn, she's fast for a baby. She got a chunk of avocado stuck between her tiny fingers, and it ended up in her nostril faster than I could say, "No! Bad baby." I didn't know what else to do. Thankfully, I was able to wipe most of it off before she inhaled and got green goop lodged in up there.

I'll have to be more careful. *And I have to buy something to suck goop from the smallest nostrils I've ever seen.* I'm just glad I wasn't eating something like peanut butter. What if she's allergic? The baby book says Fia won't be ready for solid food for eight more weeks and that there's a whole process to introducing foods to make sure you don't kill the little suckers. Thankfully, by then, Marli will have come back.

I hope?

I can't afford to buy anything else. The baby wash, diapers, and formula I ordered for delivery tonight set me back over eighty bucks. Eighty! I'm literally giving up real food for the week so I can pump fake milk into an eating machine that rewards me with poop. Seriously, changing diapers is the kind of hell that makes me question the sanity of every person who ever had a baby.

I'm never going to eat a Snickers again. Or anything brown. But at least I've learned putting tissue paper up my nose helps. Also, putting a trash bag down on the bed makes cleanup easier. Dressing her is pretty simple now that I've figured out how to maneuver those fat little arms and legs into her pink leotard thing.

See. This parenting thing isn't so hard.

Okay. Except when it comes to sleep. I'm so wound up about how I'll make it through this week that I couldn't get a nap in. Which makes the problem of not having a sitter-plan feel worse.

I fucking hate not having a plan. Sitting around with a problem isn't my style. Unfortunately, how I feel doesn't matter right now because I can't miss practice.

"Sorry, baby, but this is my only option." I load Fia into the passenger seat of my white Ford pickup.

"You're okay, right?"

She shoves her chubby little fist against her mouth and gnaws with her toothless gums. Babies are weird.

"Fine. You're good. But how about the seat? Did I put it in right? Is this how Mommy does it?" The firefighter guy online made it look so easy.

How did anyone survive parenthood before the internet?

Fia coos.

"All right, girl. We're ready for liftoff."

I get in and drive us to the stadium, going ten miles per hour under the speed limit, which earns me the love and affection of every driver behind me. They decide to express their emotions by honking and flashing their brights. *People are so rude.*

"Can't you see I've got a baby here!" I yell at one guy who flips me off as he passes illegally. "Asshole!"

I glance at Fia. "Oh. Sorry. You didn't hear that bad word."

The rest of the drive, I'm grinding my teeth, thinking about how Coach is going to react when I show up with a visitor. I'll have to convince him this is a one-off thing, and that I'm being a good player, someone he can be proud of, for bringing Fia to practice. The alternative would be leaving her home alone—something no good or sane person would ever do.

I park in the big lot next to the locker room entrance and leave Fia in her car seat so I can carry her more easily.

I get to the big steel door and pause, mentally preparing myself. The guys inside are going to give me so much shit for this.

I look at Fia. "Don't listen to a word they say, okay? They're idiots—totally the type you'll stay away from when you're older because you'll be too smart for them."

Fia doesn't comment.

"Okay. Here goes." I jerk open the door, go past the corkboard wall filled with flyers and school announcements, and enter the big room with a line of benches in the center. It smells like old shoes, Axe body spray, and Pine-Sol. The lockers around the perimeter of the space are painted black and red, our team's colors.

I make a beeline straight for the back, toward Coach's office. I think I've safely made it past everyone until one of the guys notices me.

"Look, everyone! Norland's a mom! Did you grow a pussy, too, dude?" he says.

Thank God that's not possible. I'd never leave my bedroom.

Another offers, "Wow. I know some like 'em young and dumb, Norland, but that's a little extreme."

Sick.

And finally, my favorite slam, "I like it, nanny-man. Not like you were going pro anyway."

Harhar. Funny. We bust each other's balls on a regular basis, so I know it's all part of the locker room fun, but I'm not in the mood today. I go straight for the jugular.

"Gosh, boys," I say in a girly tone. "If only I had a shrimp dick like you, I could be someone." That shuts 'em up every time.

Why? It's a guy thing. Pecking order goes: hottest girlfriend, best car, size of bank account, and then size of dick. I don't have a girlfriend or a cool car, and I'm broke as fuck. But I win anyway. It kills them. "My dick will be signing autographs after practice!" I wave my middle finger in the air. "Suck it, clowns!"

Boos erupt as I enter Coach's office. He doesn't notice me right away. Mostly because he's got a receding hairline, which he always covers with a baseball cap. Right now, his big frame is hunched over a pile of paperwork. Behind him, the wall is covered in recognition plaques. All real. He's won six national titles for Alabama and Texas. O State hired him four years ago, hoping to improve their rankings. So far, it's working. Kind of? We were number eleven last year in the College Football Playoffs. If I hadn't fucked up, we would have ranked top three. Maybe higher if we'd had the chance. It kills me that I blew it for all these guys. They were depending on me.

"Hey, Coach. Got a sec?" I say.

He lifts his head, and his blue eyes zero in on

Fia. His face turns an angry red.

"Before you say anything, Coach, it's my sister's baby. There was an emergency, and I'm the only one who can watch her this week."

"Are you yanking my fucking chain, Norland?" He slaps down his pen. "We don't allow babies at practice, on the field, or anywhere else."

My neck heats, and my back muscles tighten. Stress. "I wouldn't have brought her if I had another option."

"Ever heard of a sitter, son?"

"I didn't have time to line one up on such short notice." Not like I've got a roster of qualified babysitters lying around my apartment.

He rises slowly from his desk. He's about my height (six two) and a similar weight. Only, his girth is in the paunch. Mine is in my ass, thighs, chest, arms, cock—okay, it's everywhere but my gut. What can I say? Nature gave me a lot to work with.

"Then put her in a fucking daycare for a few hours!" he roars.

I almost lose my temper, probably because I didn't get a nap. Also, he's being a condescending prick.

"I can't afford it, Coach," I say, muting my irritation. "You know I can't." He's perfectly aware that we scholarship guys don't get our living allowances until next week, and even then, it's not a lot. My paid internship money went toward rent and food for the summer since the scholarship only covers me during the school year.

"Sorry, son, but you can't bring *it* here. Go home. Figure your shit out." He sits back down and returns to his busywork.

I turn to leave. This is bad. I'll get marked down as missing practice. He and I both know that's not allowed unless there are extenuating circumstances. Not having a babysitter isn't one of them.

I can't just leave. I stop in the doorway and turn to face him. "So what if she were mine? What if I were a single dad, Coach? Are you saying the university wouldn't support me, while they *do* support mothers—single mothers especially? Because if that's the case, I think a lot of people would be interested in that story. They'd want to hear how you're making me choose between my career, which is linked to my education through my scholarship, or breaking the law by dumping a helpless baby at my empty apartment."

He leans back in his chair and folds his arms across his chest. "Well? Is she yours?"

"What does that matter?" I ask.

"If she's your niece, then this is a babysitting issue, and you'll get no sympathy from me, considering you just threatened to blackmail me. If she's your kid, then yes, there are policies in place to make accommodations when it comes to childcare. Especially since the on-campus daycare doesn't open until next Monday—I know because I used to take my own kids there. So I would be forced to consider that a factor. So which is it, Norland?"

Fuck. Fuck. Fuck. I really don't want to tell Coach the truth. He's not going to think highly of me knocking up some woman I met in a bar, the kind of woman who'd just abandon her baby. It looks bad all around. "I'm the legal guardian for the time being?"

"Son, that's not an answer."

It sure isn't. "It's complicated?"

"Norland, that's a Facebook setting. Is it yours or not?" he growls impatiently.

I look down at Fia in her carrier. If I say she's mine, I'll avoid getting a mark against me. I really don't have a choice.

I clear my throat and meet his infuriated gaze. "Yeah, she's mine. I just found out about her yesterday when her mom dumped her at my place and took off for the week. There was nothing I could do."

Coach shakes his head. "Sonofabitch, Norland. Didn't anyone teach you to wear a condom?"

Is he going to try to shame me, too? Rude. "If I were your daughter, would you say the same? Because it's a little late for the contraception lecture." I jerk my head at the baby.

"Hell yes. This isn't 1950, son. These days they're practically handing out rubbers in kindergarten. Safe sex is branded into your tiny male brains from birth. There's no excuse for unwanted pregnancies."

I refrain from pointing out that even the safest birth control methods aren't one hundred percent effective. (A) I doubt he'll appreciate hearing my collection of personal stories related to my giant cock and how it has been known to bust through condoms. (B) He wouldn't understand, being a small-cock man himself. Yes, I've seen him shower in the locker room. There was some event he needed to attend after a game, and he had to clean up. Let's just say his gear isn't impressive. But he does have a really hairy crotch and a huge nut sack to hide his small dick, so there's that nightmare going for him.

As for me, I have been through a few condom malfunctions, so I'm no stranger to full STD workups. All clear. But sometimes it sucks being well endowed. *Kidding. It's fucking awesome.*

"Yes, I should've been more careful, but not much I can do about it now. She's mine for the week." I exhale slowly, trying not to stress out over the fact I have no game plan. I am a sad little planless man, a single-dad-ship without a rudder. "I'll do my best with the childcare arrangements, Coach, but I'm at the mercy of my friends since I can't afford much." I add hastily, "That doesn't mean I'm not committed to the team, though."

"Dean," he says sternly, "this is college football—one step away from the NFL. If you want to win, you have to be one hundred percent focused out there." He points in the direction of the field. "You leave your personal crap at home or don't bother coming."

"Are you saying you want me to quit because I'm too broke to afford a paid sitter? You know I'm on my own." The entire world knows the sob story from the ESPN spotlight—the kid from Hard Knocks who got himself a full scholarship. No family other than the troubled little brother he raised. *And a sister I just made up.*

"I'm saying we all have complicated lives— ungrateful kids, neighbors who steal your cable, a bossy wife who critiques your lovemaking on an Excel spreadsheet because she's an organizational freak. Really gets under my skin. But I have to leave that garbage at home, and you can't bring an infant to practice."

Shit. He's sending me home.

"But I'll allow it this once," he adds.

The anxiety drains right out of me. "Seriously? Thank you, Coach. I'll find accommodations for her by tomorrow." Both Nina and Lara said they could sit for me in the evenings.

"Good. But, Norland, let's get one thing straight: You're on shaky ground for last year's fuckup. If your heart's not in the game, quit now. Because the chance you're getting is taking up space."

He means that someone is always waiting on the bench for their chance to be in the starting lineup. "I'll figure it out, Coach."

"Good. Now get your ass out there on the

field."

"What about Fia?" I ask.

"It'll be a good exercise for the team. They can take turns holding her. Maybe for once they'll learn a fucking thing about not crushing everything in their path. Sometimes winning takes a lighter touch."

I chuckle nervously. "Let's hope?"

CHAPTER SEVEN

Practice goes like shit for the first twenty minutes. I mess up every single play because I'm too busy trying to keep an eye on Fia, who's being passed around like a toy between my teammates on the bench.

Yes, they all got the basic rules first—support neck, no kissing, no squeezing, no throwing her around like a ball. But a few minutes into things, I see two guys, Jarod and Wendall, playing smoochie face and blowing raspberries on her belly and neck.

Fia's squeals of delight echo across the field. Very distracting. Also, cute.

"Come on, guys. Stop slobbering on her, wuddja?" I yell. "She's a baby, not a mouthguard."

They all laugh, and Coach blows his whistle at me. "She's fine, Norland. Head in the game!"

Shit. "I know. I know." I hunker down, fist planted in the soft green sod, ready for the play to start.

"You can't even handle your grown-ass junkie brother, man. What the fuck you doin' with a baby?" says Daryl, my teammate to my right.

He's never been a fan of mine, and I don't expect him to be—not after my massive fuckup last year—but...

"Why you talking trash, D-bag? I'm here, aren't I? I'm playing."

"You call that playing?" he throws back.

The play is called, and I break away from this enlightening conversation to rush toward the sideline and make a sweep behind the skirmish team's defense.

I'm almost to the second yard line, ready to receive the pass, when I'm hit with a blow to my memory bank. A flashback.

It's *that* night. The lights are blinding. The fans are cheering. Every major sports channel is here broadcasting our game, and I know the world is watching, judging, hoping I'll live up to the media hype. People get excited about new young players who promise to break records, bring the wins, and shake things up. I never felt like *that* guy, but the university's PR team painted a picture of "Dean Norland." Handsome, smart, determined. I even came fully equipped with a touching story about the kid who turned poverty into triumph.

They ate that shit up.

But the pressure, the fucking pressure was like having my balls in a vise.

Could I play well? Hell yes. Was I capable of competing in the NFL? Absolutely.

But that wasn't the issue.

I think I didn't know how to handle the spotlight. Remember, I was the guy who grew up eating white bread and peanut butter. On a good day. No one cared if I went hungry to make sure Flip ate first. No one cared if I cried myself to sleep every night until I was twelve. And, definitely, no one gave a shit when I stopped crying because I was too worn out to feel anything at all. Getting positive attention was never in my playbook.

As I'm running, I realize how *that* night eleven months ago was triggered by all the people cheering me on. And now, *right* now, my heart can't take it—reliving that moment.

A sharp pain shoots through my chest. "Fuck!" I stumble and fall. The pass flies overhead, but I don't care. The jabbing pain is unlike anything I've ever felt—a thousand kabob skewers through the heart. I like kabobs, so that's a weird analogy. I mean, who doesn't enjoy bite-sized meat and vegetable chunks served on giant toothpicks?

My teammates rush over, but I can't see straight.

"Aaah!" I scream, pressing my hands over my heart.

Someone calls for our medic, who is always on standby. Coach is over me, trying to make me talk, but I can't.

"My chest," I groan, "hurts…"

"He's having a heart attack," Coach says. "Tell

Chuck to bring the crash kit."

Chuck is one of our EMTs.

"Just hang on, son." Coach slaps my cheek.

Whatthehell? How's that supposed to help?

"Try to breathe," he adds. "Try to stay calm."

Calm? Calm? I'm giving birth to an alien. It's busting through my chest wall as we speak. "Fia. Where's Fia?"

I don't know why I'm more worried about her than myself. I'm the one dying. Maybe because I know she'll be all alone if I die. She'll end up in foster care. With strangers. It's a total crapshoot after that. Some people are really good, but the bad ones are worse than bad.

"She's fine, Norland," says Coach. "Just worry about yourself, kid. Did you take anything? You juicing? Doing snow? Bingeing Ex-Lax for an upcoming photoshoot? Tell me now before the paramedics arrived, and I can help you manage the story."

What? "No!" I grunt. "I didn't take anything." This boy is one hundred percent corn-fed beef. Meaning, I eat a lot of chili with corn chips. What can I say? It's cheap and high in protein. "Promise you'll take her. Don't let them hurt her."

I can almost hear the gasps, followed by murmurs from my teammates. Here's the thing, the biggest reason I don't get much pity from them: I'm not the only one who had it rough as a kid. Some bounced around in foster care, some were raised by single mothers who broke their backs to give them a chance at a dream, and others had a nice life on the surface, but behind closed doors? Let's just say that bad parents come in all shapes, sizes, and income brackets.

I'm not saying that everyone on the team attended the school of Hard Knocks. Lots of guys were raised by loving parents who supported their dreams. All I'm saying is that there are enough dudes on the team who didn't have that, so when I say, "Please don't let them take her," they get it.

"We got you, man. We got you," I hear one of the guys say right before Chuck arrives with the crash kit.

CHAPTER EIGHT

"A panic attack?" I stare at the ER doctor, a thin hippie woman in her forties, wondering how much weed she smoked before coming to work tonight. "I don't panic. And it felt like my chest was ripping open."

She places a firm hand on my shoulder. "We ran the bloodwork. We did the EKG. Every indicator of a heart attack is missing. Which means you had a panic attack. I'm going to give you a referral to a therapist who specializes in your particular situation."

"Situation?"

"Playing sports is tough on the mind, too, Dean. You might want to start paying attention to signs of stress. It'll only get worse if you go pro."

If I go pro. Great vote of confidence. But I guess right now, the entire world is on the fence about me, considering how I buckled under the pressure last year. *And again tonight.*

I run a hand through my short hair. "I'll be fine. I just have to work out a new situation that popped up."

"Ah. The baby. Everyone's talking about that."

They are? Before I have a chance to ask what she means, an alarm is going off somewhere, followed by a "code blue" over the intercom. "The nurse will be by shortly with your discharge papers and follow-up recommendations."

She disappears, leaving me scratching my head. *I can't believe I had a panic attack.* Then again, I did feel under attack. Maybe my mind made a full-blown assault on my body. *But what was it trying to tell me?*

I go back to the moment that triggered me: memories of the night I fucked up last year. There were lights, cheering fans, and an overwhelming urge to flee. But why?

Fans had cheered me on before in other games, so why was that night different?

I give it some thought. *Maybe because I wasn't just another player on the field for once.* I felt like they were all there to see me play.

"Jesus." I clench my fist over my heart. Just thinking about it makes my chest tighten.

Maybe the doctor is right. I do need therapy. But whoever heard of a person being triggered by too much adoration? I can't think of anything lamer. It's like being too rich, too happy, or too good looking.

"Norland, how you feeling, son?" Coach walks in, holding a bag, and I immediately notice he's alone. "I brought the clothes from your locker."

"Thanks, but where's Fia?"

"Don't worry. She's with my wife at home. You sure that baby's yours? She's damned cute."

"Funny. And thank you. It was nice of you to take her."

"If you'd called before practice and explained the situation, I could've helped you figure out a solution, son."

I honestly didn't think of that. "I thought I could figure something out on my own. Obviously, I failed."

"Well, the team and I really admire your balls and dedication—jumping in to care for a baby you didn't know you had."

"Yeah, well, I guess that's life. Curveballs."

"And you stepped up like a champ, an example to young men everywhere of how to take responsibility for their actions."

I don't want to be an example. I just want to play football. Which is why I am not keeping Fia, no matter what. "Thank you, but I really don't plan to raise—"

"The team started a fund for you. They all put in money to help with daycare cost and diapers and all the other stuff you're going to need."

"They did?" That's really fucking nice of them.

"Yes, sir," Coach says. "And I called in a favor over at the local station. They're running the story on the ten o'clock news, but the guys already started posting on one of those social media places—Instabook or Twittgram or whatever. Donations are pouring in. You're a real example to the community, Dean."

I can't seem to talk. Mostly because Coach just said people are giving me money to help with Fia. But what will everyone say when they find out I'm not keeping her? Either Marli is coming back, or Fia goes into the foster system. *They'll all hate me. They'll skin me alive with bad PR.*

"I can tell from your expression, son, that you're overwhelmed with gratitude." Coach smiles, and the nurse comes in holding a packet of papers. "I'll be out in the waiting room. I can take you by my house to pick up Fia. Igor already drove your truck home."

"Um, thanks, Coach."

"You bet, kid." He leaves, and I hear him mumble, "Sure is a damned cute baby."

So, in other words, he doubts she's mine. *Well, same boat here, buddy.*

The nurse starts unhooking me from the monitors. "It's really great of you to take on fatherhood like that. I don't know what I'd do if someone just dropped a baby on my lap." She flashes an appreciative, doe-eyed smile at me.

Dammit. She thinks I'm some hero. I'm not. I haven't taken on fatherhood. I just kept a baby alive for a day.

She goes through a bunch of instructions about my diet—stay away from caffeine, alcohol, and any form of stimulants. Get plenty of sleep. Drink fluids. Follow up with the therapist.

I thank her, and she leaves so I can dress.

I slide on my jeans and dig out my cell from my front pocket. I type my name into the search engine, and my story immediately pops up.

Oh God. It's worse than I thought. In a matter of hours, my "situation" has gone viral. "Twelve thousand dollars?" I swallow hard. That's the amount of cash people have donated.

Why? Why are they doing this? It's just so…fucking nice!

My chest starts to tighten uncomfortably. The room starts to spin. I lie back down on the gurney and press the red button to call for help.

CHAPTER NINE

I'm released from the hospital late that night with a prescription for mild anxiety and a strong lecture from the ER doctor to make sure I go see that therapist.

Fia stayed with Coach since there was no point waking her up to drag her to my place in the middle of the night. He says they'll drop her off first thing tomorrow.

The next morning, I'm in bed, waking up later than normal. Physically, I feel fine, but there's no denying I've uncovered an issue. I'm allergic to kindness or affection or good attention, whatever you call it when people want to shower you with niceness for no other reason than they *think* you're awesome.

I'm far from awesome.

Yeah, sure, I work hard for the things I want. I'm loyal to my brother, a guy society's written off. I take my responsibilities seriously. I do not believe in leaving things to chance or allowing circumstances to define me. All good traits.

But I have plenty of bad characteristics, too. For example, I don't like complicated, which includes relationships with women. I don't trust easily. I don't like being put up on a pedestal. I'm just a guy doing his best. And—

That's it. The epiphany hits me like a head-on collision with a linebacker. *It's the whole pedestal thing.* That's what my trigger is. I can't handle the pressure of everyone treating me like I'm perfect when I'm not. I don't want their adoration because it feels like a lie. No, I have no problem with being respected as an athlete, but a pedestal takes it to a whole new level.

I grab my phone from the nightstand to assess the latest developments in my situation. If I'm lucky, my story will die down in a day, and I can get on with my life. As for the money, no one says I have to take it. I can quietly return the funds. Right?

My eyes scan the latest headlines. *What the…?* *"Young college football player becomes insta-dad with surprise baby. Team, community, and university rally to help him afford daycare and diapers."*

This made the national news?

I fling my phone somewhere on my bed and scrub my face with my hands. *Fuck. Now I'm definitely on a pedestal.* How the hell did this take on a life of its own in one day? And according to this article, the donations are up to eighty grand. Thousands of people have given. Major fucking pedestal happening.

No. Nooo. Don't think about it. Do not do it. I'll pass out if I do.

Beer. Cardio. Jerking off—I try to think of everyday things that relieve pressure instead of creating it.

The wave of tension melts from my chest. I sit up and sigh. That was a close call, but I did it. *See, you got this, Dean.* I simply need to stay focused. I'll have to maintain strict control over my emotions going forward, and everything will be fine. No more meltdowns on the field.

I hit the shower, knowing I have a long day ahead. I need to buy books, call Flip, schedule that therapist appointment, and confirm Lara's taking Fia tonight.

While I go downtown with the mountain fresh bodywash—a man's balls can never be too clean—my mind shuffles through my to-do list. Honestly, none of the items sound enticing except for talking to Lara. I kinda can't wait to see her.

I finish my shower, towel off, and give her a call from my room while I dress.

"Wow, if it isn't dad of the year," she says.

My hackles rise. *Pedestal alert. Pedestal alert.* "Let's not insult all the men out there who've suffered sleepless nights and invested years of their lives being good fathers."

"Agreed. But can you explain how you're trending as hashtag Hot Daddy Dean and the internet is exploding with a pic of you and Fia?"

So no mention of my panic attack. Guess that's a plus. "One of my teammates probably posted it."

"Well, they are getting one thing right."

"Yeah? What's that?" I ask.

"Your stepping up to take care of her—no questions asked—is pretty awesome."

I groan.

"What?"

"I'm not a hero," I say tightly. "I'm just watching her until her mom comes back, which I know she will."

"You sure?"

"Have you seen Fia?" I say. "Who wouldn't come back for her?"

"She is pretty damned cute. Kind of Gerber baby meets cherub. She's lucky. My cousin Riley was so ugly they nicknamed him Cheese Log."

Mean. "Why?"

"His face sort of looked like a long rectangle, almost like a brick of Velveeta with lips and eyes. Except he always had snot crusted on his nose—allergy condition—so I guess they thought he looked more like cheese covered in nut chunks."

"Poor kid."

"Naw. He's normal looking now, but wow, the looks he got when he was a baby. No one wanted to take his picture. But Fia, she's like a sweet little yummy gumball you just want to gobble up."

"Does this mean I shouldn't ask you to sit for her tonight because you'll try to chew on her?"

"Maybe. But I promise to stick to the toes. Baby toes are the cutest."

Okay... "I hadn't noticed. Mostly because I'm usually trying to get formula in her mouth or shit off her butt and vag—"

"Thank you, Dean. I get it."

"What? You said you're going to sit for me tonight, right? You might have to get in there and do some extreme cleaning. By the way, why did nature give girls so many cracks and crevices? Seems a little unhygienic to me. I had to give her three butt baths in the sink yesterday." It's a full-time job keeping her clean.

"You're actually making me feel skeeved out about my own body right now."

"You? I doubt there's a place on your body I wouldn't kiss or lick." *What the hell am I saying?* I can't be flirting with her.

"Nice segue into a suck-up there, Dean. Yes. I can sit for you."

"Thank you. I appreciate it."

"Which other nights will you need me?"

I give it some thought. Nina said she could help out. Unfortunately, both Lara and Nina have day jobs, and my to-do list is growing. I need to get to the gym. I also have to put in some hours at the Ranch and go shopping for supplies for Fia. They delivered my groceries last night when I was out, but she needs socks and something warmer than her leotard. So yeah, I'll need someone to watch her in the daytime for a few hours this week. I could use some of the donations—just a few hundred bucks— to pay for daycare a couple of afternoons.

I hear a knock at the front door. It's probably Coach dropping off Fia.

"I'm not sure yet. Can I get back to you?" I say.

"Sure."

"Thanks. See you around five. I have to go." I end the call, feeling unusually anxious, but in a good way. *Baby's here!*

I rush to the door and find Coach's wife. I know who she is, since she goes to all the games, but we've only exchanged a few hellos over the years.

"Hi there. I have a special delivery," she says with a smile. There's a pink backpack slung over one shoulder, an empty car seat hooked over an elbow, and a bundle of squishy wiggles in her arms.

My eyes meet Fia's, and a wave of relief washes over me. I hadn't realized I'd been feeling stressed over being away from her. Not that I think Coach and his wife wouldn't do a good job of sitting, but accidents happen. No one is going to be more careful with the baby than me.

"Hello, ma'am. Thank you so much for watching her." I step aside to let her in.

"Call me Jo."

"Yes, ma'am—I mean Jo." I reach for the empty car seat to help free up Jo's arms. She's a thin brunette with short hair, probably mid-fifties like Coach.

We go to my sparsely decorated, but clean, living room, and I set the carrier on the beige carpet.

"How did Fia do?" I ask.

"Great. I had to go to the store and get a few supplies, though. You didn't bring a diaper bag to practice."

Oops. Rookie move. I scratch the back of my head, feeling a little embarrassed. I brought one spare diaper and some wipes to practice yesterday, but I left them in my truck. "Yeah, I don't actually have a diaper bag. I guess I'm kinda new at this."

"So I've heard. It's a really great thing you're taking on." She smiles, beaming at me, and I wish she wouldn't. I feel my body rising toward that pedestal. "Which is why I've taken the liberty of stocking a backpack for you."

Just then, Jo hands Fia to me. Her teeny lips form into a smile.

"Did you see that? She smiled at me!" The tension in my chest instantly melts away as I settle her in my arms. "Hey, did you put lotion on her? She smells kinda sweet." I give her hair a little sniff.

Jo chuckles. "Boy, you're a goner."

"Huh?"

"Never mind. No, no lotion." She slides off the backpack and unzips the front pocket. "There's a supply list right here. If you make sure you've got these items before you leave the house, you'll be in good shape. Oh, and be sure you always have a clean supply of pacifiers. Once she starts eating solid food, you'll need to include the items on the back of the list—snacks, juices, extra sippy cups, baby spoons, etc."

"Wow. Thank you." I like being prepared, so a fully equipped diaper bag is definitely a good idea. But did she have to make the backpack pink? I'll look stupid carrying that around.

"Don't mention it," Jo says. "Happy to help. Our kids are all grown now—no grandkids yet either—so it was nice getting my baby fix. She's wonderful, by the way. Such an easy baby."

I didn't know there were different kinds of babies. I figured they all just sleep, eat, cry, and shit.

She adds, "I gotta run, but if you need anything, just give me a call, okay? I left my cell number on the bottom of that list—always have emergency contacts in the bag, including her pediatrician. That way if someone sits for you, they know who to call if you're not reachable."

Oh. Another good tip. "Thank you. I'll have to add that pediatrician number once I get a doctor for her."

No. Wait. I'm not keeping Fia. I know I can't take care of her. It wouldn't be right to pretend otherwise. I'll be on the road, at practice, or in class every second of every day until December—if our team does well this season. When I'm not doing that, I'll be sleeping or trying to study. I also have to put in a few hours every week at the Grape Ranch.

No time for a baby.

And despite the public's kindness, money doesn't change anything. You can't just leave a baby with strangers, in daycare or with a sitter twenty-four seven. It's like getting a dog and leaving it at a kennel. Not really fair to the dog.

Not that Fia is a dog, but if she were? Not cool.

I walk Jo out, and she gives Fia a quick kiss on the cheek. "See you, baby girl. Make sure you tell your daddy to take it easy. He's gotta take care of himself, too."

She means I can't run around having panic attacks. I'm sure Coach told her.

Jo leaves, and I take Fia to my room. She feels so wiggly and warm. "So what would you like to do today?" I ask her. Her big gray eyes go wide, and she makes a funny little "ba" sound. "Oh, you want to take a giant crap and have another bath? I bet you would, my sweet little turd factory."

"You can't call a baby that, man." Mike appears in my doorway.

"You're home."

"Yeah, in between girlfriends again." He shrugs like he couldn't give a shit.

"Sorry to hear that, man."

"I'm not. I like to keep the door revolving. Makes things easier."

He hates attachment. I get it. "Since you're not busy, want to help me do some shopping? Fia needs a bathtub, some socks, and probably some warmer clothes." Even if Marli comes back, these are all things she can use. "And that portable bassinet is a joke. I need to get something that doesn't take an engineering degree to assemble."

"Sorry. I have a date with the gym."

I scowl. "Come on. Don't make me go baby shopping alone. I need a baby wingman." I've never been in a store for infants, but I get the feeling it'll be like going to the tampon store. I won't have a clue what I'm doing.

"Fine. I'll go, but don't ever call me baby wingman again, and you owe me."

CHAPTER TEN

Mike and I are in the truck with Fia, driving to Baybeeland, when my phone rings.

Mike answers for me and says it's the local news station requesting an interview. I don't know how they got my number, but apparently, they want me to come by the station so they can present a surprise: A local daycare facility is donating a hundred free hours of care. They want to promote their establishment with single dads, stay-at-home dads, etc.

Wow. Kindness is practically falling from the sky. Donations, help from Coach and Jo, Nina and Lara, and now this?

"I really appreciate it," I say, "but my schedule's packed." Really, I just want to avoid any more pedestal situations. Also, I haven't driven down to visit Flip lately.

He actually left a message last night while I was busy having a panic attack. It slipped my mind until now. I guess I got distracted with Fia.

I make a mental note to call Flip back before practice. I know he's been having a rough time with the rehab program, and it's probably because half the people are only there due to court mandates. The last time he went in, he came out with a long list of new friends who had zero interest in staying clean. They did their time and went back to using or dealing. Flip was no different.

Part of me wishes I could use all the donations for him—get him somewhere that can really get through to him. I found a place in Nevada that might work, but it's private. One month costs over thirty grand, and I know Flip; he'll need to be there three or four months, plus there's an outpatient program. It's money I don't have.

Mike relays the message and then comes back with, "They say they can meet us at the stadium before practice. It'll only take five minutes."

I could use the help, for sure. Even if donations are rolling in, I don't plan to keep all the money. Or maybe I'll find a way to ensure that money stays with Fia no matter where she ends up.

A tiny tick of sadness pulses through my heart. I've only had her a few days, but I'm already worrying. What will happen to her if I'm not around?

"Sure, yeah," I say. "Tell them to meet me there at a quarter to five. But it'll just be me." I can't take Fia to practice again, and there's no reason to plaster her face all over the news.

Mike says they agree and ends the call. "Man, if I knew people would act like this, I would've gotten me a baby a long time ago."

I frown. "Funny." Sad part is, with the way Mike whores around, he probably already has a few kids somewhere. He claims he's only responding to the fact he grew up in a small town where the pickings were slim. And unless you wanted someone's pissed-off father showing up on your doorstep with a shotgun, you didn't mess with people's daughters. Here in Oregon, he feels free to play the field, even if, as he says, the chicks are generally too weird for his taste. "Take it from me, Mike, figure your shit out before you go having kids."

"Dude, you've been a dad for two whole days."

Not entirely true. I've been a dad, a bad one, since I was ten. "Exactly. If I know after two days how hard it is, that says something."

Two hours later, Mike and I are back from our shopping expedition. Dear God, I never knew so much baby stuff existed. They had special feeding pillows, electric trash cans to wrap dirty diapers, toys that light up to make your baby smart (or super crazy), tons of books, bottles, clothes, food, and strollers with surround-sound, Wi-Fi, and a wine fridge. Fine. That last one is an exaggeration, but not by much. Some high-tech gear out there. My head nearly exploded, and Mike was no help because he met some woman over in the breast pump section. *Fucking Mike, man.*

Anyway, I told the saleslady I needed the basics aside from what I had in my bag. She set me up with more bottles, a bottle cleaner, bib, diaper rash cream, easy-access snappy-crotch baby long johns—or whatever they're called—and a bunch of other stuff.

Man, was it expensive. After I threw in diapers, extra formula, and the travel crib, the shopping trip set me back six hundred bucks.

I've never spent that kind of money on anything. Except maybe a lawyer for Flip.

"Lucky girl. You got all the fancy stuff," I say, making room for her baby gear in my closet.

Fia makes a warning whimper—almost like crying but without the commitment. I decide the best course of action is to head off the imminent hangry meltdown and make her a bottle.

I already texted Lara early, who says she can get off work early and come over, which is great since I need to get to the stadium ahead of time.

There's a knock at the front door just as I'm sitting down to give Fia her bottle. Igor surfaces from his room, looking grumpy. "I veel get it." He probably went for a long workout and was resting up before practice.

"Thanks, bro."

A minute later, Nina's cheery voice and pretty face are blessing my living room. "Hello, famous Hot Daddy Dean!" She's wearing her team uniform—the shortest shorts I've ever seen and a skintight tank top.

Yes, there is a God. I can see the lines of every muscle in her arms, abs, and legs. She's definitely a lean woman who works hard at running, which I respect.

"Hey, I was just about to give Fia her lunch. Or snack. Or whatever meal this is. She eats ten times a day."

"We both know those protein shakes aren't very filling." Nina smiles, beaming at my pink little ball of baby cuteness.

"You want to feed her?" I ask.

"Oh, uh…sure! Let me wash my hands."

Nina goes to the kitchen sink and returns, plopping down next to me on the sofa. I hand the baby over.

"Oh, you do look hungry." Nina pops the bottle in Fia's mouth, and damn me if I don't start getting a little swoony. Not that guys like me swoon, but if we did, it would be over this hot runner chick holding my baby.

Whoa! I jump to my feet.

"Everything okay?" Nina asks.

"Um, yeah." I point over my shoulder. "I, uh, I just remembered I was supposed to turn in some online forms for football. You know, injury waivers and that kind of stuff."

"Go ahead. I can handle this."

I go to my room, shut the door, and double

over, panting. I just called Fia "my baby," and I kinda meant it. Or felt it? Whatever. Point is, I said the words in my head without really thinking. That means something, right?

What the hell is wrong with me? I take a deep breath and try to slow my thoughts. Then I look down, glaring at the fly of my jeans. *Have I grown a pussy?* Because I'm feeling all maternal today. Next thing I know, I'll be filling out compatibility surveys in *Women's Magazine* or complaining about sore nipples.

I scrub my hands over my face. *Get a grip, Norland. Get a grip.* But I definitely started feeling an attraction to Nina just now. Seeing her holding my daugh—*the baby*—lit up my heart.

Several minutes later, I'm feeling calm and collected again when I hear the door followed by Lara's voice.

She's early.

I walk out to the living room and find Lara in tight-ass jeans and a white blouse. Her blonde hair is loose around her shoulders. She looks insanely hot. Well, from below the neck, anyway. Above the neck, she looks irritated—tight lips, furrowed brows, narrowed eyes zoomed in on Nina.

"Hey. You're here," I say.

"Yeah, Hector said I could go early. You haven't called him yet, by the way, and you probably should. He's going to be hurt when he finds out the entire planet knows about your baby sitch and he doesn't."

Crap. I did forget to call. I also haven't called Flip yet. This isn't like me to forget things or flake on responsibilities. I like my life orderly and under control.

"I'll go see Hector as soon as I can," I say.

"Good. So, you going to introduce us?" Lara asks with a bite to her tone, flicking a finger at Nina.

There's no missing her eyes taking in Nina's "swimsuit." But that's the uniform for track. What can I do?

I glance at Nina, who's still sitting on the couch. Fia looks like she's in seventh heaven, clasping the bottle with her fat little hands and sucking away.

"Lara, this is my neighbor from downstairs, Nina. Nina, this is my coworker from the Grape Ranch, Lara."

The two women exchange smiles.

"So do you still need my help tonight?" Lara sounds pissed, and I'm guessing it's because she took time off work to be here.

"Oh," Nina steps in, "I was just stopping by to check in after practice today. Wanted to see if Dean needed anything."

I can tell Lara is annoyed, but what's with the jealousy? She and I are just friends. Yes, I like her. But like I've said a million times, me and complicated don't get along. Women are complicated. Relationships are complicated.

"That's really nice of you, Nina," says Lara, who then looks at me. "So should I go?"

"No. Please no. I definitely need your help tonight," I say.

"I can stay if you want," Nina offers. "I've got nothing else to do."

Lara looks back at me, and I'm feeling the pressure. Why? What the hell have I done wrong?

"I, uh, well…" *Think fast, Dean!* "I could really use both your help this week. So much going on. Lara, would you mind helping out tonight as planned? Nina, would you be okay with covering me during practice tomorrow night?"

Both women agree with a smile, but I'm sensing an undertone of bitterness. I can't handle this right now.

"Okay, so…I'll just get my stuff ready for practice." I leave the room, shut the door, and start to sweat. The kindness is crushing me.

Stop, dude, you're being dramatic. I really hate complicated. I do everything in my power to steer clear of it.

After about ten minutes, there's a light knock at my door.

I wince, dreading it might be more drama with my name on it. "Yes?"

"Hey, Fia's done with her bottle. I think she needs a change."

I open the door and see Lara standing there holding a stinky baby, with her eyes watering from the smell. "The odor already ran Nina off. Says she'll text you later."

"Sorry. I'll get that." I take Fia in one arm and dig through the pink backpack on my bed for that changing pad. It's a lot nicer than the roll of trash bags I have on my nightstand.

I quickly do the diaper deed, imagining I'm somewhere safe and warm, holding an ice-cold beer and maybe smelling coconut suntan oil. Before I know it, Fia's all clean and wrapped up nice and tight like a tamale. If that tamale had a putrid-fudge autofill setting.

"Wow. I'm impressed," Lara says, watching me like a spectator from the bleachers.

"Thanks. The internet has videos on everything. Hey, do you mind holding her for a sec? I have a few minutes before I have to leave for practice, and I want to set up her portable crib." The lady at the store showed me how to do it. Eight easy steps.

"Sure."

I hand her over, and the two start giggling while I get to work. Lara is making smoochies on Fia's neck. Once again, I find myself mesmerized. Lara would be a natural as a mother.

"God dammit!" I bark at myself. *What's the matter with me?*

Fia starts to cry.

"What's wrong?" Lara asks. "Did you hurt yourself?"

"No, I-I…" I turn and look at Lara. I want to

lie to her, but I can't.

"What, Dean?" she pushes.

"Nothing. Today's just…things are…difficult lately."

"So you decided to randomly scream and curse and upset your baby?" She puts Fia's head over her shoulder and starts rocking her back and forth while administering a soothing back rub.

"Would you stop that?" I grunt.

"What?"

"It's distracting me."

"What's distracting you?" Lara continues the back rub.

"The mothering."

"Why?" She frowns like I've lost my mind.

"Because…" I can't say it.

"Dean, I'm your friend, remember? I promised no judgment."

"Fine. I think it's sexy watching you hold her."

"What?" She bursts out laughing.

"You said you wouldn't judge," I snarl.

"Sorry. Sorry. You caught me off guard."

"Trust me, you're not alone. I really don't get what's happening to me." I sound like a damned lunatic. My emotions are all over the map. I'm forgetting things. And now, I'm really liking watching Lara hold Fia.

"Babies make us see the world differently. It's a normal part of becoming a parent. It's also normal to enjoy watching someone dote on your baby."

"I didn't say I enjoyed it. I said it made you look sexy. Is that normal?"

Lara smiles bashfully, pushing a lock of golden hair behind her ear. "Sure. Why not?"

"Are you sure, because you're not a parent."

Lara gives me a look.

"Wait? Are you?" I ask.

"I am—was. But I don't like to talk about it."

Too bad because I really want to ask what happened. I decide it's better not to pressure her. "I'm really sorry. I mean—it's none of my business—but I'm sorry if what I just said flicked off an old scab."

"'Tsokay." She waves a dismissive hand through the air. "Can I suggest something, though?"

"What?"

"Do you trust me?"

I don't trust anyone. I shrug noncommittally.

"Good enough," she says. "Lie down on the bed and put Fia on your chest."

"Is this some sort of mommy and me exercise?" I saw a video online.

She points to the bed, and I obey, lying flat on my back. "Bring it on."

Lara lays Fia facedown on my chest. Baby is full, dry, and kind of all limp like cooked spaghetti, so I think she's ready for a nap.

"Good, Dean. Now close your eyes, put your hands on her back, and just feel her breathing. Feel her heartbeat against your chest."

I do as Lara says. It's weird, but I instantly feel

relaxed. The rhythm of Fia's soft tiny breaths, the pulse of her heart, and the amazingly sweet smell of her hair. It's like an instant tranquilizer.

"What do you feel?" she asks.

"I guess I feel…good."

"Do you feel like you'd do anything for her? Say a person broke into your apartment right now and wanted to take her. What would you do?"

My eyes fly open. "I'd fight them."

"See. No one ever told you to feel protective of her. They didn't have to. The instinct to love and care for her is just there. In your heart. It makes sense that you'd gravitate toward people who feel the same way." Lara sits next to me.

"Do you like when I gravitate toward you?" I ask.

She blushes but ignores my question. "Stop judging yourself for how you feel."

I *feel* like ending this conversation. Lara just brushed me off. Also, I need to get ready for practice. Unfortunately, the warm weight on my chest is making it difficult to escape. This is the most relaxed I've ever been.

I inhale slowly and enjoy the feeling. Fia is like a magical creature. She controls everything around her, including me. I just wish I knew how all this is going to play out. I have my plan, but what if it's wrong? What if handing her over to Marli or Child Services isn't best for Fia? What would happen if I kept her?

"What if I fuck things up?" I ask, thinking out loud.

"Not possible. As long as you listen to what's going on in your gut, Fia will be okay. You just have to trust that."

I give it a long moment of thought. What does my gut say?

"I'm terrified of being like my mom," I blurt out, completely shocked once the words leave my mouth. I never talk about Mom to anyone. It's too painful. But with Lara, the words just came out.

"Good," Lara says. "Worrying means you're aware, and that'll keep you from repeating whatever your mom did to you."

Lara doesn't know the full story. No one really knows except Flip, and sometimes I wonder if even he understands what I went through. I had to keep our situation hidden for years. I had to make sure we ate, stayed clean, did schoolwork, and packed lunches. I had to make it seem like a responsible adult was at home, taking care of us. To this day, I'm still shocked that no one caught on. Everyone just believed my uncle was a crappy guardian who couldn't cook. Peanut butter sandwiches or Vienna sausages for lunch every day.

After a few long moments, the baby drifts off to sleep. "I don't want to wake her, but I have to go," I say.

"She's not a bubble. Fia won't pop if you handle her when she's sleeping. In fact, my mom always made tons of noise when we were babies—ran the vacuum with us strapped to her back. She did dishes, put the TV volume a little higher, and did her normal stuff. She claims we were able to sleep through anything no matter what." Lara picks up Fia without any fanfare. The baby whimpers for a moment and then conks out again. "See. Just make noise and movement part of the routine. They get used to it."

I want to ask how she knows so much, but I don't want to pry. I figure Lara will tell me when she's ready.

I force myself from the bed, noting my heavy, relaxed limbs. Even my joints feel looser.

I stand and face Lara. Funny, I always thought she was beautiful, but now I feel like I'm seeing her for the first time—the pronounced dip of her upper lip, the cluster of freckles on the tip of her nose, and... *The way she's looking at me.* It's more than desire. It's electric.

"Thank you," I say.

"Sure. Anytime, Hot Daddy Dean." She flashes a smile, and I don't know what comes over me, but I lean down, careful not to touch the baby, and I kiss Lara. Her lips are soft and warm and feel surprisingly wonderful. Familiar, too. It's like I've kissed her a thousand times. *And I still want more.*

Shocked, I pull back, and she blinks up at me. "Don't start something with me unless you really want it, Dean. I'm not...into casual." Her eyes dart away.

In an instant, I know that kissing her was a mistake. *What the fuck, Dean? What's your rule about complicated?*

Lara is basically asking me not to start something unless I mean it.

And I don't. I'm not in the market for a girlfriend. At the moment, I'm trying to make it through the week without getting attached to a baby who isn't mine to keep.

I step back, putting distance between us. "You're right. I'm sorry. I don't know what comes next for me, but it's not a relationship." I have to take care of Flip first. I have to take my shot at going pro. I have to get through college. And I absolutely have to make it happen.

She nods, looking wounded—eyelids heavy, corners of her sweet mouth turned down. "I get it."

"You want me to call Nina?"

"No. I'm happy to watch Fia." She reaches out with her free arm and squeezes my biceps, sincerity gleaming in her soft brown eyes. "I'm here for you, Dean. No matter what. Whatever you need."

She must be a saint to put up with me and not run for the door. "Thank you."

"Sure." She nods solemnly and disappears to the living room with Fia.

By the time I leave for practice, the porta-crib is all set. I go to tell Lara, but she's asleep on the couch with Fia on her chest.

I try not to let the image get to me, but there's something about the loving picture that reminds me of my childhood, of always wanting a mother. To me, they were fictional characters, only found in sitcoms on the old crappy TV we had.

Listen to yourself. You're actually standing here getting the warm gooeys, staring at Lara and Fia. What's next? Shopping for yoga pants?

I leave for practice emotionally tapped out. I know tonight my body will be in the game, but my head will be here at home with these two.

CHAPTER ELEVEN
LARA

When I wake, Dean is gone and Fia is still snoozing on my chest. Looks like she had a long day of shopping. I set her down in the porta-crib Dean put together next to his bed.

A tiny teddy bear with a pink bow is propped up in the corner. I remove it, because better safe than sorry, but I can't help smiling.

This man perplexes me. In the best kind of way.

I met him back in June, when he started as an intern at the Grape Ranch. Of course, I tripped over my drooling tongue the minute he walked through the door. The guy has stunning hazel eyes and is built like a giant oak. Meaning, you could climb him for fun, but swinging from his branches might be awesome, too.

But what really made me take notice was his energy and confidence, of the way he filled the room when he entered. The Dean-cherry on the top was that he didn't seem to notice how women turned into puddles of hot syrup in his presence. It perplexed me—the effect he had.

That was the beginning of the end for me. I couldn't stop thinking about him. He became a puzzle I wanted to solve. What was it about Dean Norland that made my insides turn into a fluttery mess every time I got near the guy? I'm not talking butterflies. I'm talking helicopters flying around in my stomach.

After days, weeks, and months of Dean-think, I came to one conclusion: When it comes to looks and his body, he's a perfect ten. But that's not the secret sauce. Dean's off-the-chart sexiness comes from the fact that he's unapologetically himself.

Yet, at the very same time, when you talk to him, you get the impression he's wearing armor. And lives in a fortress. Surrounded by a moat. Filled with alligators.

Ask him where he's from, he deflects with, "Nowhere worth mentioning."

Ask him what he plans to do after football, he says, "Die of boredom."

Ask him if he'd like to hang out, grab a bite, he says, "Thanks, but I'm on a strict diet."

Don't get me wrong, Dean is absolutely kind and polite. His smile is a panty dropper. But he keeps everyone at arm's length, especially anyone who's into him. Me, for example.

That's why when I learned of the baby situation, I was thrown off. *Dean? Taking care of a baby?* He's the type of guy who buries his emotions and enjoys lifting heavy stuff—which we ladies at the Ranch really appreciate.

He's also smart—knows a lot about wine and catches on quickly to pretty much everything Hector asks him to do.

Dean is driven, responsible, and respectful of women, too.

But playing the role of daddy? I couldn't believe it.

Then I caught a glimpse of him beaming at Fia…

Nothing has ever made my heart go *awww*…like that. The joyful twinkle in his eyes, like he was melting into his own ooey gooey puddle of baby adoration, made me melt right along with him.

I've been getting to know Dean for months, and my serious case of like is now a full-blown case of need, desire, and admiration. Seeing him with Fia was the nail in the want-him-now coffin. My stomach actually hurts from the ache.

My biggest problem is the very thing that just made me fall for him—Fia—makes it impossible to be around him.

I can't do it.

It's just too painful to be near that sweet, adorable baby. Even after all these years.

Yes, I said I'd help him, and I will try to keep that promise because I wish someone had been there for me when I needed help. Still, that doesn't change how I feel. I don't know how much longer

I'll be able to keep up this lie and pretend I'm okay with being a part of his life.

I glance down at the sweet little baby girl in her crib. "I'm sorry I'm so fucked up. Because you are perfect, little one. And so is your daddy."

I go to the kitchen and start preparing for the rest of the evening. Better to treat tonight like a job. *Don't get emotional. Focus on the task.*

NINA

I can't believe Dean. He doesn't have a clue about how I feel, does he?

I'm such an idiot. I've been running around like a lovesick puppy ever since he moved into my complex. I mean, look at the guy. He's tall, ripped, and totally charismatic—but not in a gross cocky way. He's more of the quiet, strong type.

And those eyes… (Insert image of me fanning face.) Hazel has always been my thing, but his eyes are like sexy mood rings. Some days I could swear they're forest green with gold flecks. Other days, they're a rich warm brown with olive-green speckles. And when he's between your thighs, his eyes are just…*intense.* Which leads to my other point: his dick.

Wait. Let me back up before I go there.

I met Dean at their housewarming party—really just a bunch of their football teammates and a few people from our complex. I showed up with my roommate, Kimmie, because she said some hot guy named Mike invited her, so I had to be her wing bitch. Fine. I owed her one. Plus it had been months since I'd touched a carb. Or a dick. So, yeah. Free beer. Maybe score an orgasm. Why not?

I'd just chopped off all my hair for practical purposes, so that night, I made a special effort to wear something extra girly and sexy. My flat chest and lean, boyish frame often mislead guys into thinking I'm into chicks. Nope. I like dick. I like muscles. But I also love to run. I love to work my body to the point of exhaustion.

Anyway, I dressed in a short skirt, tight tank top, and sandals. Red lipstick and silver earrings punctuated my fashion statement. Statement: Let's fuck.

Ready for action, I walked into Dean's place and wasn't disappointed. An ocean of tall, muscled men lay before me, and any one of them would do since I was only after a good time.

Then I saw Dean.

He was standing by the keg, surrounded by four girls. All pretty. All giggling and batting their eyelashes. Couldn't blame them. He looks like a long-lost Hemsworth brother, but with short dark hair and shoulders you could build a treehouse on. *Yummy.*

But what really got my attention, besides his incredible looks, was the fact he wasn't flirting back.

He just stood there, being a polite host, nodding respectfully at the girls as they chatted away. I figured maybe he wasn't into women.

So disappointed, I thought. *The hottest ones are always gay.*

Later that night, I found him on his balcony, sitting alone and chilling with his phone, reviewing plays for some upcoming game. Long story short, we got to talking about athlete life, had a few beers, and he made a move. No one was more shocked than me.

And let me tell you…

It.

Was.

Amazing.

His lips. Wow. The way he kissed, like he was hungry for my touch. How his big strong body moved over mine, like he savored being inside me. And his hip action, like he really took my pleasure seriously. No rapid releases with this guy.

Yes, and now we get to the part about his dick.

At first, I thought I was hallucinating. Then I panicked a little. My fingers could not close around his velvety hard shaft. Way too thick. As for length, well, images of a prize-winning cucumber at the state fair come to mind.

Give that man a gold ribbon, ladies!

I didn't just see fireworks when I came, I saw my entire life flash before my eyes. I saw dancing bears, singing birds, and every kind of happy cartoon animal known to man. Magical.

The next morning was where I blew it. I'd never actually had the urge to spend more than one night with a guy, but Dean had me livestreaming all sorts of fantasies in my head.

So yes, I fled back to my place. Biggest mistake of my life.

A few days later, he showed up at my door, and I was thinking, *Yes! He's back for more! He's into me.* Because, honestly, I hadn't been able to stop thinking about him.

Nope. He was not coming for seconds.

"Hey, um," he said. "I just want to apologize for the other night. I shouldn't have let it go that far. I'm really not in a position to date anyone right now. But I didn't want it to be awkward when we see each other around the complex."

I agreed because what else could I do as his words crushed all hope from my soul? He was the first guy I ever really liked.

"Sure. Yeah. Cool. I run track, so I totally get it. Sports come first," I lied. That philosophy was the old me. After my major burnout from training for the Olympics, I had a coming to Jesus. Success is nothing if you're killing yourself to win. I'd been out of control, and I was never going back.

Something clicked with Dean, though. I was willing to fake how I felt to get more of it. "I'm glad you get it. Not many people do," he said.

After that, two things happened: One, he started

popping by to vent about some game he'd screwed up. Honestly, I saw a few news articles, but the "career hara-kiri" he claimed to have committed wasn't so obvious to me.

One bad game. Big fucking whoop.

Pro teams invest in stats. They invest in potential, demonstrated by year over year improvement. For example, I can't walk onto a football field, kick a goal, and get drafted by the NFL. Athletes have to show what they're made of, and sometimes what the scouts love most is seeing how a player bounces back. Because, let's face it, we all screw up. All players have horrible games or seasons. The pro scouts want to see how quickly and successfully the person picks themselves up and gets back to business. But that's Dean's downfall. He's a perfectionist, in it to win it.

All he needs is the right woman by his side to help him realize his potential and not sweat the bumps in the road. He needs me.

As for point number two, I got to thinking how most guys would never come to your door and tell you to your face that a hookup was just a onetime thing due to life's circumstances.

But that's when I really fell for him. He's honest.

Dean is also hardworking, smart, really intense, and kind. But he's incredibly tough on himself. Every mistake, every second he doesn't spend pushing himself is a failure in his eyes.

So here I've been, being the patient friend and sounding board for his career. I figured if I just hung in there, he'd eventually see how much we have in common, that we could be a great team.

Then this baby comes along.

What the fuck? A baby, Dean? Dude, you have a future. I have plans. She is not a part of it.

Of course, I can't say that to his face without coming across as a coldhearted bitch, so my only move is to continue being the steadfast friend. His loyal woman "friend." The one he leans on for advice.

If I play my cards right, I'll make him see that he's got a big bright future. With me. The two of us—not three—conquering the world.

So who the hell is this Lara chick?

Well, luckily for him, I'm also in it to win it. I'm not about to let almost a year of time invested go down the drain for a baby and some dumb slut from his work.

Game on, honey.

DANNIE

My friend Quincy and I are sitting on the red couch in my living room, celebrating with skinny margaritas.

"I can't believe Dean Norland took our free daycare offer!" I squeal. We just opened our flagship daycare facility five months ago. It's bursting at the seams, and a second location is already in the works. The idea is to target young, successful, single parents who fall into the extreme-workaholic category. We plan to expand into three more states by the end of next year. After that, franchising. That's where the money is.

My goal is for Green Babies to be the McDonald's of daycare. *If McDonald's had no carbon footprint and cost thirty bucks an hour. Cha-ching!* Parents will get uniform quality no matter which facility they bring their kids to. No need to screen, interview, or waste time getting recommendations from friends on where the best places in town are.

Why?

Because we do all the work.

Every employee will have the same training, background check, and unreactive temperament— certified by a DNA test to screen out those with an undesirable genetic history. *Anyone who's into privacy need not apply.*

Every location will use our environmentally friendly products and have the same sanitation protocols, along with a low child-to-adult ratio. All sites will come equipped with a 360-degree video feed in every room so parents can check in on their kids at any time. We'll also provide a holographic chat station so parents can remotely interact with their offspring during those long twelve-hour days at the office. Or the herbal enema spa. Or the psychedelic mushroom retreat in the Amazon jungle—a must for the young entrepreneur.

Hey, success is stressful. Which is why we offer peace of mind and a fully integrated remote parenting experience.

Ah, nothing like technology-enhanced neglect.

Not that I'm judging parents. I don't even have kids. But I went to an Ivy League business school and did my research. After an entire two weeks—*brutal!*—of rigorous online hashtag searches and following every single-parent influencer under the sun, I came to the conclusion that the market was wide open for a one-stop-shop, fully cloud-integrated, child-management system geared toward working single parents.

Duh, right?

Because everyone knows that marriage is *so* last century. Co-parenting is more the norm. *Blah. Where's the independence in that?* Personally, my social compass is pointed toward a mass migration to a single-parenting model. Total freedom from the heavy. No pressure to appease a partner as to how a child should be raised.

The parent of the future wants value, quality, and prestige. They want assurances that their children are safe, but also carbon neutral. They want the Tesla of daycare. And I'm here to deliver. Green Babies Daycare.

God, that sounds so good when I rehearse it in my head. I really have my sales pitch down.

"So what's our next step?" Quincy asks. She's one of three co-investor buddies who moved to Portland with me. We figured it was the ideal place to test out our business model. We have two other active investors in Seattle, the site of our second location. We are all single. No interest in marriage. Because…who needs men? Am I right? They're just dicks with half a woman's brain.

Kidding. They have a quarter.

But don't get me wrong; we women definitely need men. Just not for marriage or to father our kids. Sperm banks were made for a purpose.

Can I get an amen?

Because personally, I want to control the when, where, and how I have a baby. I want a complete genetic workup of DNA, too, when the time comes. Until then, my only interest in the opposite sex is for the orgasms.

'Cause nothin' like a hot cock to release the tension after a long week of building a billion-dollar empire to serve the masses who hate the idea of family as much as I do. It only holds you back.

That's right, Dean. And I'm pressure cooking right now. Can't wait to test you out.

"The next step?" I smile and sip on my cocktail. Dean's already taken the bait. Once he brings his baby to our daycare, we can use that to create some online buzz. Hot Daddy Dean is our newest client. But we don't plan to stop there. "Now we make Dean the spokesperson offer, as discussed. In fact, I think I might stop by his place tonight so I can introduce myself and make the offer in person." And by that, I mean I want to fuck him. Honestly, I don't know what I like more. His tall, ripped body or his face. There's just something about the sensual shape of his lips that turns me on.

"Should I come, too, since I'm your partner?" says Quincy.

"I think it's best you let me handle this on my own." I pat her thigh.

"You think he'll sign on?" she asks.

If not, he's taken our donation for one hundred hours of daycare for his surprise baby. It's already a win because all the dads out there will see this big pile of muscles admitting that he needs our brains to raise his unwanted kid.

"Who cares? The single dads will eat it up." Especially after our ad runs during the big O State game on Sunday. Let's just say I'm the face of my company for a reason. Big lips. Big tits. Tight body. I spend two hours each morning doing extreme yoga—you know, where you balance on a cliff or atop a boulder. It has to be somewhere dangerous. Of course, I'm not stupid, so I use the 3D experience at my gym.

"So you're not going to push for a deal with Dean Norland?" Quincy asks. "You know how I feel about deviating from our five-year business plan. We need someone like him to increase enrollment. And he's perfect for our brand. Have you seen the public's response to him?"

I know. He *is* perfect. But I make it a point to not need any man. In my personal or professional life. "I'll make Dean the offer." *And then I'll fuck him a few times.* "If he turns us down, we move on to the next candidate." *I'll fuck him, too.*

Honestly, what else are these dumb jocks good for?

"Okay, Dannie. But like we agreed, you don't make a move or change in our plans unless we all agree."

"Of course, sweetie. I would never disrespect your role and the value of your opinion." *Just as long as you don't get in my way.*

CHAPTER TWELVE
DEAN

What the hell? After practice, I pull up to my apartment complex around eight thirty, and I'm greeted with several news vans.

Are they here for me? God, I hope not.

I already gave one interview for the local news, right before practice. Actually, it was more of a photo op. I was presented an oversized gift certificate, and the reporter made a plug for the daycare facility that offered me one hundred hours of daycare. It was over in sixty seconds. Alternatively, practice dragged on forever because I couldn't stop worrying about Fia. She was left in capable hands, but I was still chomping at the mouthguard to get home.

I park my truck at the side lot of my complex and take the back stairs to my apartment. If those news vans are here for me, I want to avoid being seen. I'm anxious to find out how things went with Fia. Also, there's the whole pedestal thing I'm working through. News equals attention I might not want.

I'm almost to my front door when I spot a woman in tight jeans and a snug black sweater. She has long dark hair, dark eyes, and deep olive skin. She is drop-dead gorgeous. Also, I have a thing for brunettes. I think because my first porn was a video called *Grecian Babes of Grease. So much baby oil. Mmmm…*

I slap my juvenile sex-pumped thoughts away and get back to the issue at hand: the hot woman in spiked heels strutting toward me. She's flipping her hair, swinging her hips, and puckering her cherry-red plump lips like she's giving a performance.

Oh, look. Here's me wanting to hand out an Oscar. I'm watching every move, feeling my chest puff out and my cock thicken with thoughts of spending the night with a tasty vixen who looks like she'll outsmart me, chew me up and spit me out before I've even come.

I do love a little danger. I love a challenge more, and this girl brings it all. *Plus, a bag of glitter.*

"Hi, Dean. I'm Dannie. Can I *come* in for a minute and talk? I have a business proposal."

I stare like a rabbit in the crosshairs of a hunter. If that rabbit really wanted to hump said hunter.

"I'm Dean," I say like a brainless moron.

She laughs. "Yeah. I know, cowboy. So is that a yes?"

I shake my head and try to snap out of my lust-fog. "Wait. Who are you?"

"The free daycare. Green Babies? I'm the owner."

It's a little strange that she'd show up at my place like this, but who am I to complain? She's brought material for my wank bank.

"So," she jerks her head of silky straight hair toward my door, "can I come in? Or do you want to talk out here and get mobbed by all those reporters looking for fresh video footage of the hot dad of the hour?"

"Yeah. Sure." I'm about to go inside, but then I remember Lara and Fia are inside. "Actually, the baby might be sleeping. What if I come by Green Babies tomorrow? I can bring Fia. You and I can fu-fu-talk."

Wait. What am I thinking? Oh, that's right. I'm not. I am in no position to date, hook up, or otherwise. No new plates. My current ones are still spinning, but barely.

She flashes a predatory smile. "How's seven a.m.? I can show you around our establishment."

"Seven's great." I can leave Fia for a few hours, hit the gym, pick up my books, and stop by the financial aid office. In the back of my mind, I make a note to call Flip, too. I still haven't had the chance. "Hey, but, if you don't mind, what is this about?" I'm curious.

She leans in and whispers in a muted voice, "I'm going to change your life."

She is? "How?"

"How's a hundred thousand dollars sound for a few hours of your time?"

For sex? Wait, no. This lady is hot. She can get sex for free, including from me. "To do what?"

"We need a face for our growing company. And you, Dean, have quite the face." She winks.

I'm about to change my mind and invite her in when the door opens. Lara is standing there with a dish towel over her shoulder and white stuff down the front of her shirt. *Baby vomit.*

Lara sneers in my direction. She probably wants to get going.

Meanwhile, Dannie doesn't even acknowledge Lara's presence.

"See you in the morning," Dannie says.

"I look forward to hearing more about the offer," I say.

I watch Dannie walk off. I'm blinded by lust, but there's no ignoring the quiet nagging voice in the back of my head. She's a shark. Is this really what I need in my life right now?

On the other hand, one hundred thousand dollars for a spokesperson gig is exactly the kind of help I could use. With it, I could get Flip into that private facility.

"Hello? Earth to Dean. You can put your tongue back in your mouth now," says Lara. "Dean? Dean?" She grabs my elbow and gives it a squeeze.

"Sorry. What?"

Lara shakes her head. "You've got to be kidding

me."

"What?"

"Never mind." Lara goes inside, and I follow.

"Did I do something wrong?"

"Nope." Lara goes to grab her purse. "Fia had a bottle about thirty minutes ago. She went down to sleep five minutes ago. You're welcome." Lara sails past me, heading for the door.

I reach for her wrist to stop her. "Wait. Why are you mad?"

She jerks free and points a finger in my face. "You need to get your head on straight, Dean. That little girl is counting on you."

"She can. And I'm doing my best." It's only been a few days.

"Do better. And a word of advice? Don't make people wait around, taking care of your kid, so you can line up your next fuck."

"I wasn't lining up a fuck. That woman is the owner of…" My words fade off because Lara is out the door.

Crap. And she's right. I was thinking with my dick. Actually, no. I wasn't thinking at all because my dick was too busy dancing around the giant bonfire of lust that Dannie woman just lit.

Still, Lara is right. I have to do better. If that Dannie wants to make a spokesperson deal, I should have it flow through a lawyer. Yes, I'd still like to try out the daycare, but I can't afford to get pulled into a bad deal just because that woman is hot and she could probably talk me into anything. Also, I should be more careful whom I invite into my life.

I park my thoughts. I can deal with all that in the morning, including apologizing to Lara, though I'm not sure why I have to. She and I are not in a relationship. We are not going to be in one either. I find her attractive more and more every day; however, she's my friend and coworker. I'd be stupid to add a Lara plate to my table.

But maybe a nice fuck? "No. Stop it, Dean," I mutter to myself.

"Stop *vhut*?" Igor saunters in through the front door, also returning from a long practice. "Oh, did *choo* know there are many reporters out in the parking lot? They want the big interview with the 'hot daddy.'"

Great.

Igor goes to the kitchen to make his usual dinner—some fish recipe he loves that stinks like hell.

I go to my bedroom and see a tiny little person sleeping. I instantly forget about my long crazy day. Yeah, I do need to try harder; even if I'm not sure what's going to happen with Marli, I kind of do want to be a part of Fia's life.

I just wish it didn't have to be such a small part.

Reality is, even if I kept Fia, which I'm not saying I will, when would I see her? How would I have the time between football, college, and work?

Of course, if I'm drafted, I'll probably have to put college on hold. I'll have to relocate to whatever city takes me. I'd be on the road for a good part of the year.

I know plenty of pro players have families, but I wouldn't be able to take care of a baby on my own. Even with a really great nanny, the kid would be raised by strangers. Wouldn't a foster family and stable home environment be better? Or maybe things between Marli and her ex will work out.

My mind quickly throws out all the things I hate about those two options. Foster care is still a crapshoot. Some are great parents, I'm sure. Others are not. As for Marli, would I really want her cheating ex raising my daughter? And what kind of mother just abandons her baby like that? She's either incredibly selfish, or she's unwell mentally. Neither are good for Fia.

Fuck. I run a hand through my sticky hair. I need a shower. And I need to figure this out. More and more I'm beginning to see that I might be Fia's only option.

I just can't see how it'll work. Not unless I give up football. And college. Both?

No, I can't. I refuse to give up after I've worked so hard to get here. I'm this close to either having my formal education or getting into the NFL. If I quit now, what sort of future will I have?

No chance in hell am I going back to a life of poverty. And that is exactly what Fia would get if I threw in the towel on all my plans just to take care of her full-time. Or even part-time.

Bottom line, the pieces of this messed-up puzzle don't fit. And I hate every single option on the table.

I don't know what to do. I only know how I feel. Or…am starting to feel? Like I can't just dump this little girl off on someone else's lap. She's my plate. I have to spin it.

So which other plates do I drop?

CHAPTER THIRTEEN

The next morning, Fia is a ball of energy. She's kicking her legs and making the funniest noises—like little "yippees!"—the entire time I'm trying to wash, dress, and feed her. "Someone's in a good mood," I say.

Must be all the TLC she got from Lara last night.

I think of Lara and instantly feel crabby. She promised to support—not judge me.

And why's she getting so upset anyway? Yes, maybe there's a little something between us. An attraction. An easiness when we're together. Yes, she is the type of woman I would date. If I had time for dating. But attraction is fleeting. Lara and I have friendship. I think? Whatever we have, I can tell you what it's not. A committed relationship.

My mind offers up how I got all warm and squishy inside—so unmanly—when I saw Lara sleeping with Fia in her arms.

Ah! But I got a little tingle when I saw Nina holding Fia, too. So clearly, the tingles aren't exclusive to

Lara.

So then why is it bugging me that Lara left here angry last night?

I push the mental junkyard off. I have too much to do today before practice, so I can't afford to get distracted. Tonight, Nina will watch Fia, and tomorrow I can deal with the Lara thing.

I grab Fia's backpack—damn this pink thing. So lame!—and restock it. I love the checklist Jo made for me, though. Very efficient.

Soon, we're off and arriving to Green Babies Daycare at seven twenty. I'm late. I hate being late. It's unprofessional and shows a lack of discipline.

Nothing I can do about it now.

I'll go in, drop off Fia, and get on with my day. I've already decided to hear Dannie out, but any further discussions will have to go through our lawyers. I can't afford one, but tonight I'll ask some of the guys if they know anyone reputable who could help me out. I can pay them after everything's done.

Either way, I won't be staying long at Green Babies. I'm not interested in Dannie and need to take care of a bunch of things, including stopping by the Grape Ranch.

Hector texted me last night and asked me to come in. He probably found out about the baby and is pissed because I didn't tell him. I'm hoping he's not going to fire me. My hours were going to be limited during football season anyway, but I need the credits for the internship requirement. The cash is always welcome, too.

After that, I've still got to get my books for next week, check in to see where my scholarship funds are, and then, hopefully, I can get some quality time with weights at the gym. It's not enough to go to practice. I have to stay in perfect form to play well and reduce the likelihood of injury.

Crap. I still need to call Flip back. It'll have to wait until this afternoon.

I walk into Green Babies Daycare, pink back-pack in one hand and Fia in her car seat in the other. There's a long bright red counter at the entrance, and behind it is a sort of giant glass child terrarium. You can see the space goes back a ways and is divided into clear cubicles.

"Hi. Welcome to Green Babies Daycare. May I help you?" says the guy behind the counter, who can't be much older than me. "Oh. And who do we have here? Isn't she a doll."

Don't even think of touching her, dude. I'll smack you. "I'm here to see Dannie."

"Sure. One sec." He picks up the phone, and Dannie appears a few minutes later. She's looking hotter than hell of course. Black jeans. Tight red sweater with a green baby on the front. It's hideous, even if it shows off every curve of her body.

Nope. Nope. Not looking. I'm here to do busi-ness.

"Well, well, Dean Norland. So nice to see you

again. Won't you please come to my office?" She beckons me with her index finger.

"I'm only here to drop off Fia. I've decided your offer needs to go through the proper legal channels."

"Oh. I see." She flips her long straight hair over one shoulder and offers a cordial smile. "Well, I can't say I blame you, Dean. We're offering a lot of money, and you're smart to want the right eyes reviewing the fine print."

"Glad you understand." *See. That wasn't so hard, was it?* I got straight to the point. My brain was fully engaged.

"Sure. No problem. Can I give you the tour since you're here?"

"I'd like that." I leave the pink backpack from hell on the counter and take Fia in her car seat with me. I follow Dannie as she shows me all the sanitation protocols and the cameras and introduces me to the staff who handle infants.

"Babies are kept in their own enclosed room here. We feel it's important to have an extra layer of security. Do you know how many babies are stolen each year?"

Who would want to steal a baby? They're a crap ton of work. "I don't know."

"Thousands. That's why we have additional security, though the main room has its own safety protocols, too. And each employee undergoes a background check that could rival the CIA."

"I suppose it's smart to make sure the people

watching your kids aren't terrorists."

"Each employee knows CPR and has had first aid training with annual refresher requirements and…" Dannie goes on and on about all the bells and whistles, playtime, feeding schedules, etc. By the time I've had the complete sales pitch, my head is spinning.

"So what do you think?" she asks.

"Considering my criteria was that you keep the baby alive for a couple of hours, you've exceeded my expectations."

She laughs. "You're funny."

I wasn't trying to be. My only goal these past few days was to not lose, maim, or accidentally kill this baby. It's a lot harder than people think. "So can I leave her for the morning? I need to take care of some things before the season kicks off on Sunday."

It dawns on me that by then Fia might not be here. Marli said she was coming back in a week. This Sunday will be one week.

My heart and stomach feel heavy all of a sudden.

"Sure, she can stay," says Dannie. "Kyle, our childcare technician up front, can take all your information and copy Fia's vaccination records."

"I don't have her records."

"Nothing?" Dannie gives me a strange look.

"No." Is that a bad thing?

"Not even a birth certificate?" Dannie asks.

"She was left on my doorstep with ten diapers and a two-day supply of formula. That's it."

"Then how do you know she's yours?"

I don't. "Look, she's mine to care for until Sunday."

"What are you talking about? The news said the mother hid her from you and then dumped her on you and walked away. For good."

"I don't know what the news is saying. All I know is I need help watching her. Today."

"But—but—we want you to stay a dad, Dean. It's part of the deal. You know, as our brand ambassador for single fathers."

What's her point? Does she think I'm going to put her business ahead of Fia? *I knew this woman is a shark.* "I have to do what's right for Fia. If that happens to fit with your business strategy, and you still want me as a spokesman, that's great. Let me know what you decide." I turn to leave, but Dannie rushes around to stop me.

"Wait. Hold on. I'm just trying to process your situation. That's all. I was…taken by surprise." She offers a warm smile and flips her hair over one shoulder. "Let's get you set up so you can take care of your busy day."

The puff of toxic steam inside my chest disperses. Maybe I was too quick to jump to conclusions. "Thanks, Dannie. I appreciate it."

"That's what we're here for, to help parents just like you. Life is messy. Children are even messier.

We can at least bring peace of mind to that part of your life."

Why do I feel like Dannie is still trying to sell me something?

She gestures toward the front of the baby terrarium. "Let's get you registered. Basic information only. I'll call our lawyer later and have her write up the terms of our offer so it reflects something more palatable."

"Sounds good."

We go up front, and Dannie gives me one last speech. "Dean, thank you for trusting us with your most prized possession. We will honor that with top-quality childcare."

What is wrong with this woman? She sounds like she's completely made of cheesy taglines. "Yeah. Sure. Thanks."

After I register Fia, I leave with an uneasy feeling in my stomach. But it's no worse than yesterday when I left Fia with Lara. I trust Lara, so I'm pretty sure I'm still not used to releasing the reins.

I brush it off and head to the Grape Ranch to meet with Hector, who says he wants to talk. When I get there, I run into Lara walking through the parking lot, coming out of the bottling building.

She's wearing a pale-yellow dress, looking like a sexy flower. Her blonde hair is up in a messy ponytail, and her lips are a shimmery pink.

Our eyes meet, and my heart starts to pound. It dawns on me how differently I feel around this woman compared to someone like, say, Dannie, where my initial attraction died a quick death. With Lara, the more I see her, the more tempted I feel to take a gamble. She just keeps getting prettier.

"Hey, Lara," I say as I follow her into the building where we have the tasting room and offices.

"Hey, player. Where's your PR prop? Leave her in the car? Closet?" She narrows her eyes and continues through the tasting room to the door leading into the administrative area. It's pretty early in the day, so there are no customers yet.

"What are you talking ab—"

"Dean. Oh good, you're here!" Hector spots me coming and waves me into his office.

I look at Lara, who goes to her desk, avoiding eye contact. I don't like it. I like the fact that she's still upset with me even less.

"I want to talk to you before I leave," I say.

"Oh? Well, I'll have to check my schedule. See if I have room for dumbasses." She swivels in her chair and taps away on her laptop. "Oops. Sorry. All filled up."

That's enough of this. I don't have the energy for mind games. "You done?" I say sternly.

Her brown eyes finally look up at me. She arches a brow, and her lips flatten.

Yeah. That's right. I just barked at you, lady. "Lara, I'm not sure what's ruffled your pretty little feathers, but if you're trying to piss me off, then keep going with this childish routine. Otherwise, grow up and talk to me like an adult." I shake my head. "I'll be back in a few."

I walk away feeling, well, like kind of a dick. I'm not sure why I said that to her. Maybe because I trusted her, even admired her. She's the last person I expected to act like a brat.

She wants me to do better? Okay. I will. I can. But she needs to step up, too, because I don't have the patience for this.

I enter Hector's office, where he's seated behind his big desk. Hector is a tall, thin man with dark, leathery skin. A large picture window with a view of the sprawling hillside and endless rows of vines is behind him.

"Take a seat, Dean. We need to talk."

CHAPTER FOURTEEN

"You're selling the Ranch?" I suspected he might be thinking about making a move, but the news still shocks me.

"I know you were considering a job here after graduation, Dean, but let's get real. We both know it's not meant to be."

"Yeah." I hang my head. "I wouldn't want to hire a weak link either."

"What are you talking about?" He frowns.

"I'm sure you've seen the mess—from last year. Now this week."

"I don't watch the news, Dean. It's a packaged reality, and I don't subscribe to any of it."

"That a monk thing?" Hector used to be a monk in France somewhere. He left for unknown reasons, but the company website says he perfected his wine-making skills during a period of "reflection and a vow of silence." I suspect a woman had to do with him going into the monastic life and him leaving it. He's a passionate man, driven by his heart.

"No." He chuckles. "Personal choice. But why don't you tell me what these messes are all about?"

"I'd rather not."

"You can trust me, Dean. I am the last person to judge you."

I've heard that before. "Why's that?"

"Because my entire life has been one screwup after another. I can hardly count all the times I've wished I've said or done something differently." Hector threads his fingers together and rests his hands on the desk. "But I've also learned mistakes come and go. It's what we take away from them that makes us worthy."

"Worthy of what?" I ask.

"Love," he says like it's the obvious answer. "Is there anything else?"

"Purpose. Honestly. Loyalty." And how about winning?

"All forms of love, tough guy. Purpose is about knowing how best to serve your fellow man, and serving others is a demonstration of love. Honesty is a show of respect—another form of love. Loyalty is the same. Anything worth living or dying for is a form of love."

I give his words some serious thought. I read a lot—philosophy, history, porn magazines. A man has needs. Don't judge. But as many times as I've encountered the concept he's talking about, I never really connected with it. Bottom line, everything I do is out of a sense of duty, not love.

"I guess I just don't see it that way," I say. "But maybe that's what happens when you're still swimming around on the bottom of Maslow's hierarchy." It's a pyramid, meant to explain how human needs influence our lives. At the very bottom is survival—food, water, shelter. The next level up is safety. After that comes belonging and love. Then esteem. Finally, at the top of the pyramid is living one's full potential. It's figuring out your purpose for existing.

The takeaway is that a person who is starving or freezing to death isn't worried about fulfilling their dreams. Personally, I've never really made it past the second tier: safety. Yes, I say football is my dream, and it's true, but that's not why I work so hard. It's because I want to feel safe from starvation, from the cold. I need the same for Flip.

"Maslow had it all wrong," Hector says. "Faith in yourself and your purpose is the foundation. It can carry you through the worst hunger, pain, sorrow, and loss. Without faith in ourselves, man would just lie down and die at the first sign of adversity."

"You know everything. Maybe you should be a self-help guru or write a book."

"Ha!" He slaps a hand on his desk, chuckling. "You actually made me pee a little in my pants."

"Gross."

"See. I'm far from perfect. For example, I've built a successful winery with international recognition. I'm going to sell it for more money than I ever dreamed of having. Yet I feel just as empty as the day I left my monastery and started this venture. I thought if I carved out my own path, God would point the way toward the happiness that's eluded me."

I don't believe in God. But I believe in Hector. He treats everyone with genuine kindness and respect. He's a role model to most of us employees. "Did He reward you?"

"I don't know yet. But during my time running this winery, I've made many new friends. Regular people, famous people, and powerful people. I've learned something from almost everyone who's crossed my path, but there is one man who stood out: a NASCAR driver. He's made a lot of headlines recently, and do you know what he said when I asked him about his secret to winning?"

"What?"

"He said that every time he gets on that track and drives those five hundred miles, traveling two hundred miles an hour, he loves every second of it. Getting to the finish line first never crosses his mind because he's having so much fun. That and it's only one one-hundredth of a second. For him, it's all about enjoying the ride, not a perfect finish that's over in the blink of an eye. He just doesn't care if he gets first place." Hector smiles, a twinkle in his dark eyes. "Yet he wins anyway. Go figure."

Hector's words make me think hard. Some people spend their entire lives focused on reaching a goal, kind of like what Nina was saying. She pushed herself so hard that it broke her. All for what? She never made it to the finish line, the Olympics, and she wasted years of her life being unhappy.

So am I spending all my time obsessed with the big touchdown? Meanwhile, there's no joy in the game I'm playing. I've never had a life. No serious girlfriend. No real fun. No close friends—only hordes of casual ones. Mostly because for as long as I can remember, I've been worrying about Flip. I love him. He's my brother. So that's not the point. But I have spent a solid percentage of my childhood and adult life focused on the finish line.

I'm trading everything just to get into the NFL. Nothing wrong with that in theory. I know plenty of guys who want it. The question is if that's the game *I* want. Will it make *me* happy? If not, then all the NFL contracts, money, and Superbowl rings in the world won't do it for me.

"So now that I've made my confession," Hector inhales slowly, "you want to tell me what's going on?"

No. I don't want to tell him, but I should. I'm beginning to realize if I want to get out of this mess, I can't do it alone.

I sigh with a deep groan. "I'm pretty sure I got someone pregnant. And now I have a baby girl. And now that I've met her, I don't think I want to give her up. But she and football and college and everything I've been working for…I don't know how to make it all work. And I feel like I should, man. I should have it all figured out because that's what I do. I'm Dean Norland. The kid from shit who said screw you to the world when they told him he'd never make it."

Hector bobs his head appreciatively. "So what will you do?"

That's a damned good question. "Honestly? I want to enjoy the five hundred miles around the track. And I want the perfect finish, too. I want it all, Hector. I want to fight for all of it."

He smiles appreciatively. "Then what's stopping you, Dean? It's your life. Just don't sacrifice the ride only to get to the toll bridge. We all get to the toll bridge, if you know what I mean."

"Yes. I do." For the first time in my life, I'm wishing I had a father. One like Hector. "Thank you, boss."

"I'll always be here for you, Dean. Even when I'm on my yacht in the Riviera, writing sad poetry about my empty life."

I crinkle my nose. "You have a yacht?"

"Yes, but it makes me feel like garbage. I'm cursed."

CHAPTER FIFTEEN

I'm on my way to pick up Fia from daycare, feeling like that talk with Hector helped put things in perspective. Unfortunately, Lara was tied up on the phone with one of our major retailers when I left, so I had to put a pin in our conversation. Maybe for the best. A cooling-off period never hurts.

Either way, my problems are still here, but that conversation was the first step in figuring things out. Adding to my optimism, it's been a productive day. Got my books, confirmed my money for school is on the way, and I've got a daycare to look after Fia until that situation sorts itself out.

Not bad for day four of daddying.

I'm even making headway with deeper issues— such as trying to separate myself from the pressures of winning races. I mean playing football. Now that I'm beginning to understand my triggers, I have a shot at conquering my pedestal hang-up. I don't need to be the perfect man. I just need to be a good one.

Speaking of good, I need to step it up in the

brotherly support department with Flip.

I hit the speaker on my phone to finally call him, but Nina's voice comes on. Her call must've been coming in at the same moment.

"Dean?"

"Hey, Nina. You still coming over to help with Fia tonight?"

"Um, Dean. Are you sitting down?"

"I'm driving, so yeah."

"You might want to pull over."

My stomach rolls and tightens into a brick. It's the feeling I get when I know something bad's about to happen. "Please don't tell me another baby just showed up at my apartment?" Or maybe it's news about Flip?

No, the rehab center would call if something were the matter.

"Just pull over," she says.

"Fucking hell." I swear, if this whole #Hotdaddydean thing turns into random women with paternity suits, I'm going to move to Mars.

I flip on my signal and pull into the parking lot of a grocery store I was about to pass. "Okay. I'm parked. What's wrong?"

"I, uh, just got wind of something trending on social media. A friend of a friend tagged me on it."

"Okay. What now?"

"Um, um…"

She's making me nervous. "Spit it out."

"That daycare place, Green Babies, is saying Fia

is stolen, that you took her from her mother as a PR stunt to help your career and get people to notice you."

What the fuck? There has to be a mistake. "Why would they say that?" Dannie was just offering me a spokesperson deal.

"I don't know, Dean. But they posted it. I checked on Twitter myself."

My heart starts to race. I'm furious. Who would do such a fucked-up thing? "I need to go. I need to get Fia."

"The police already took her."

"What? Without calling me? I'm the father." Don't they have to contact me by law or something?

"Are you, though?" Nina pushes back.

"The mother says I am."

"Then I'm sure this is just some mix-up," Nina says, not sounding the least bit confident. "Maybe she'll see the story, or the police can track her down and set everything straight."

Fuck. How's this happening? There are no words for how I feel right now. Someone took my baby!

"Or," Nina adds, "maybe the baby *is* stolen. Maybe the mother is crazy and took Fia from someone and left her with you until things are quiet enough to retrieve her. Yanno?"

That would be insane. Then again, I keep telling myself that something is really wrong with Marli. Why would she just pop into my life and leave her baby with me?

And here I am, trying to be the good guy, putting Fia first. I never even questioned all the other stuff.

"Crap," I groan. "I knew I should have called Child Services." Of course, I'm only saying that because I feel like an idiot for being sucked into a scandal and possibly being duped. The truth is I didn't hand Fia over because it wasn't the right thing to do. Not in my gut.

"What can I do to help?" Nina asks.

"I have no idea, but I'm fucked. No pro team will want me. The university'll probably suspend me, pending an investigation. And how will I show my face in public? Dean Norland, baby thief."

"Just tell the police exactly what happened. Mike was there, right? He'll back up your story."

That's right. Mike. Mike will tell them everything Marli said. Then the truth will get out. "I gotta go. I need to call him." I'll have him meet me at the police station.

"Dean, I just want to say that right now the most important thing is doing damage control. Your career, your future, everything's on the line. Let me call my old PR manager. She might have some advice on how to counteract the tsunami of bad press."

"Thanks, but what I really need is to find Fia's mom." She can put any questions to rest and get my baby back.

"Maybe this is a sign."

"What do you mean?" Because I'm really not following. Unless Nina means the world is a cruel place.

"Maybe you should distance yourself from this whole thing. It was never going to work out anyway, right? College, your pro career, *and* a baby? And what about having time for love, for a woman—someone to support you on your rise to stardom? You were always going to have to choose, Dean."

I frown, momentarily thrown off guard. Suddenly, I'm thinking about my conversation with Hector. What do *I* want?

I want it all. I don't want to give up a thing. But what if Nina is right? What if I do have to choose?

Or maybe the choice was just made for me. *If I can't fix this, my career is over.*

She continues, "Look, I'm fairly sure my PR gal will agree, but your best defense is putting the blame on Fia's mother. Hold a press conference or do an interview. Tell everyone you were tricked. This woman saw you as her meal ticket and wanted to set you up for a blackmail situation. You had no clue the baby was stolen goods."

"Nina, I can't say that."

"Yes. You *can*. You've worked way too hard to get where you are, Dean. Are you really going to throw it all away on some bitch you met last year in a bar, and a baby who's probably not yours?"

Who is this person? "I have to go." I want to say much, much more to her right now, but it's not the time. I'm swimming on the lowest rung of Maslow's hierarchy: survival. Because suddenly, I don't give a fuck if I blow my career or lose my scholarship.

I just want my fucking baby.

"What the hell, Mike? What do you mean you won't come down to the police station?" I squeeze my free hand around the steering wheel of my truck while my fingertips attempt to penetrate the plastic case of my cell phone. I can't believe what I'm hearing.

"Sorry, man, but I can't get anywhere near this," Mike says.

"Dude! I didn't do anything wrong! And you were there when Marli dropped off Fia. You have to tell the police what happened."

"You don't know where that baby came from, and now you're toxic, man. Cancelled. I can't afford to be implicated."

Sonofabitch. "Mike, I'm going to tell the truth to the police, which means you're already in this. You were there when the baby was dropped off."

"Yeah, but dude, it wasn't like I had a choice to take her. That woman showed up, said the kid was yours, and left."

"Exactly. Then just say the truth, Mike. Why wouldn't the police believe us?"

"I'm not going to admit that I took possession

of a stolen baby. That's human trafficking. I'm not getting involved. I saw nothing. I know nothing."

"We don't actually know she's stolen. And you live with me," I point out. "Don't you think everyone'll question your story? Kind of hard to miss a crying baby in your home."

"You threatening me?"

What the hell? "No! I'm saying if you lie, they won't believe you. Same for me. Which is why I intend to tell the truth. You have to do the same."

"No! No way," Mike protests.

"Stop being a pussy and step up. Do the right thing."

Mike groans on the other end of the phone. "Dean, I want to, but…"

"What?" I bark.

"My family. They won't approve."

"Approve of what?"

"Of me living with a sinner. You had a baby out of wedlock."

I'm at a loss for words. I don't see what this has to do with telling the truth to the police. "So?"

"I kinda lied and said you guys are super religious."

Seriously? So he's more afraid of his parents knowing his roommate situation isn't wholesome than he's afraid of lying to the authorities?

This is the biggest crock of shit I've ever heard.

The truth is, Mike is a coward and just doesn't want to get involved. This story about his family is an excuse.

"Mike, I *am* trying to do the right thing here. I can't let them take Fia. I did nothing wrong. Please, I'm begging you to help me here."

"You want me to fight for a baby who's stolen?"

"Stop, man. Okay? As far as I'm concerned, Fia is mine, and I want her back," I still don't understand what would drive Dannie to make such a wild accusation on social media and then call the police.

"If you go to the mats, bro, it could wreck you. This chick—the mom—could turn out to be a con artist. A baby snatcher."

"Fine. Then we'll uncover the truth, and I'll have peace of mind knowing Fia is with her real parents. But I'm not about to abandon her. I don't fucking care what anyone else thinks. And neither should you, Mike. You get how important family is."

"No. I don't. Mine drives me fucking nuts, which is exactly why I don't ever want to move back to that shithole of a small town, and why I can't leave college without a pro contract. If you want the same, you need to distance yourself fast from this shit."

He's just like Nina, telling me to save my own ass instead of getting to the truth and doing what's right for Fia.

"You want a ticket to escape where you came from. Cool. I get it. But this isn't about you or me, Mike. It's about that baby. She needs us to figure this out. If I'm her dad, then she belongs with me." It feels freeing to say it because I mean it. I really do.

"Even if it means giving up everything? Because, bro, if you don't get ahead of this shit, you'll always be known as the guy who took a baby to make a name."

I could try to turn this mess on Marli, but that doesn't solve Fia's issue. If she's really stolen, which I have no reason to believe she is, then her parents are going nuts looking for her. If she's mine, then she belongs with me—which is another set of problems.

"Yes, even if I have to give up everything. It's like that old saying—"

"If you love something, set it free. If it comes back, shoot it because it's an idiot?"

I was going to say, *You don't know what you have until you've lost it.* "You're about as funny as a crushed kneecap or pulled hamstring, Mike. I gotta go. I'll be at the police station if you decide to grow a pair and change your mind."

I end the call, feeling like I've been punched in the gut, run through a woodchipper, and fed a toxic burrito. I don't know if I want to throw up, scream, or shit myself from nerves. This whole situation is bringing up garbage from my childhood I've buried deep: worrying about the police taking us away and wondering how I was going to take care of Flip if they didn't.

I got through that. I'll get through this, too.

I restart my truck and head to the police station.

CHAPTER SIXTEEN

"And can you describe this woman who left the infant in your care?" Detective Stratter asks, sitting across the table from me in a small interview room. He's a bald husky man who got under my skin the moment I walked into the station, asking where the hell Fia was. So far, he hasn't said anything, and now I feel like I'm under arrest. Maybe the locked door and scowl on his sun-damaged face has something to do with it.

"Do you know the child's date of birth? Location of birth? The mother's full name?" he asks.

"No. But like I said, I only met Marli one time in Houston."

"And she tracked you down after eleven months?"

"Yes." Why does he insist on going over this again? I already told him my story.

"And you weren't home when this woman dropped off the baby."

"No," I reply. "I was downstairs with my neighbor Nina. My roommate Mike was home. Marli, the mother, just showed up, said the baby was mine and that she'd be back in a week. She left a note talking about reconciling with her husband. That was it."

"Do you have this note?"

"It's in the diaper bag, which I left with Fia at Green Babies. It has some instructions, too, so I like to keep it with me."

He nods, glaring with suspicion. "Uh-huh."

"If you don't believe me, have someone check."

"We will. Just like we checked with your roommate, Mike. He says he never saw this Marli woman. He claims you came home with a baby and said it was yours."

Asshole. "He's lying. He doesn't want to get dragged into this. Bad PR is a death sentence for guys like us."

"Just like good PR can help your career?" Stratter probes.

Crap. This guy already drank Dannie's Kool-Aid. I don't know how to defend myself against someone who's already made up their mind. "There are plenty of other ways to get PR that don't involve baby nabbing. And, by the way, did you ever consider the sheer practicality of a stunt like that? It would require a single man, who has college classes, football, an internship, and a brother to worry about, to also find time to care for a baby. Makes no sense."

"Tell me more about your brother."

I frown. "What do you want to know?"

"Let's not be coy, Mr. Norland. We've all seen the ESPN spotlight. Flip has been in and out of trouble for years. Those legal expenses must be piling up. And now public donations are pouring in."

Now I see where this is going. He thinks I did this for money. "I did *not* steal that baby. I was only trying to take care of her until her mom comes back. That's it."

"What did you plan to do with all the donations after she left?"

"Give it to her! I would never take the money for myself. That's why I went to Green Babies. The owner offered a spokesperson deal. I planned to use the money from that opportunity to help my brother. I won't touch the donations unless it's directly to help Fia."

Stratter doesn't even look at me. He's not buying anything I'm saying. So, basically, I've gone from father of the year to a criminal in less than a day.

"You have to look into my story," I plead. "You can track down Marli using the phone number I gave you." It was the first piece of information I passed along.

"Dean, do you have anyone, anyone at all who can corroborate what you're saying? Did you mention this woman to anyone after your initial encounter? Did anyone else see her?"

"Besides Mike? No."

"Tell me where you really got the baby."

Dick. "Her mother. Why don't you search the airline records from Houston to Portland? She didn't walk here, and Marli isn't a common first name."

He ignores me and continues pushing his theory. "Perhaps you went to your criminal brother and asked him to help you obtain a baby. For a share of the donations."

"My brother is an addict, not a baby trafficker." I can't believe this shit. It's ridiculous.

The door opens, and a man in a gray suit is standing there with another officer. Behind them both are Coach, Lara, and Hector.

"Stratter, the kid's lawyer is here," says the officer.

"Mr. Norland, don't say another word," says the guy in the gray suit.

"Who are you?" I ask.

"We've obtained legal counsel for you, son," says Coach. "Larry here will take care of everything and get to the bottom of this."

I'm completely shocked. In a good way. After how Nina and Mike acted, I thought I was on my own. Again. Words cannot describe how good it is to see these four people here to help.

"Detective," says Larry, "it is not against the law to seek care for a child. And last I checked, parents were not required to have pink slips proving ownership of their children."

Stratter leans back in his chair, cocky as ever. "We were called because there was concern for the child's well-being."

"And what alarmed the daycare exactly?" asks Larry. "Was there evidence of neglect? Is there a missing child fitting the infant's description? Has someone stepped forward claiming the baby is theirs?"

"Mr. Norland couldn't provide any information about the child."

"Because, as he said, the mother left the infant in his care to attend to a personal matter. That is also not against the law. In fact, as unorthodox as her actions were, I would argue she *was* looking after the child's well-being. I can tell you, as an attorney who's been practicing family law for over fifteen years, I've seen neglect. That's not it. So unless you can produce evidence that my client or the mother has harmed or stolen the infant, or has in any way broken the law, you need to return the infant to his care. Immediately."

Stratter is red-faced and fuming. I can see we won this battle. I'm thrilled. But I know we haven't won this war. We need to get to the bottom of this mess. For Fia. For me, too. I have to know if she's my daughter, and if not, then whose?

And where the hell is Marli? By now, she's had to have seen me on the news. So why wouldn't she be calling?

The detective says that someone from Child Services will call and arrange to have Fia dropped off at my apartment, but I can tell by his tone that he's not letting this go.

Lara, Coach, Hector, Larry and I go outside to the parking lot. The sun is finally out. Maybe it's a good omen.

"Mr. Norland, this is my card," says Larry, handing it over. "I have to run to the courthouse for another urgent case I'm working on, but call if you need anything. The hour doesn't matter. I've also arranged for you and Fia to take a blood test first thing tomorrow. If it turns out she's not your daughter, we'll need to be prepared to show you were not involved in any criminal activity. If she is yours, this test will prove it so you can start the process of obtaining full custody. You do want that, don't you?"

I don't know. Do I? Full custody is a big deal. It means I'm agreeing to raise Fia and be there for her the rest of my life. Solid food, crawling, walking, potty training, kindergarten, training bras, periods, and boys. *Oh God!*

My pulse races. My brow starts to sweat. *This is a lot.* There'll be no more telling myself it's just temporary. There'll be no more football first, Flip first, or my future first. Pursuing full custody is a formal commitment to make this baby my number one priority. And I have no clue how to do that.

Suddenly, an image of Fia's sweet little pudgy

cheeks and big gray eyes flashes in my mind. A wave of serenity washes through me, followed by a warmth in my heart. I have no plan and no idea how I'm going to make this work, but I know I want to.

I swallow a lump in my throat and nod. "Yeah. I want full custody."

"Good," says Larry. "Because if everything these three people have told me is true, and I have no doubt that it is, then it's the right move. It sounds like the infant's mother isn't fit."

"I don't know that. She could be going through a rough time." I'm not sure why I'm defending Marli, because I actually agree with Larry. I guess a part of me still hopes there's a logical explanation for all this. For Fia's sake. What kid wants to find out their mother just walked away? For me, it changed my life, and not in a good way.

"Well," says Larry, looking at his watch, "for the benefit of your daughter, assume the worst and prepare for the best—best for her. The last thing you want is for the mother to turn out to have mental issues and then come out and say you stole the child or aren't the real father."

"You think she'd do that?" I hope not.

"I've seen it all when it comes to custody battles. But the first step is determining if you're the biological father. Once we have that, you have choices, and we can figure this out. Fia comes first, though."

I couldn't agree more.

I thank Larry, and he heads to his car—a sleek silver Mercedes. I can't imagine how much hiring him must have cost.

I turn to Hector and Coach. "I don't know what to say other than thank you. How did you even know I was here?"

Hector glances at Lara, who's still in her yellow dress, looking both cute and somber. "Lara heard what was happening and called your roommate Mike. He said you were here."

"He was blubbering about being a bad person," Lara adds. "Oh. And that he would burn in hell for fucking you over." Lara looks at Hector. "Crap. I mean crud! Sorry for swearing, boss."

"'Tsallright." Hector grins. "I forgive you. And I'm glad you got me involved. Larry's an old friend and the best family lawyer money can buy."

I am incredibly curious how an ex-monk-turned-winemaker would know this, but now's not the time. All that matters is getting Fia back. Also, I'd really like to punch Dannie in her kneecaps. Not that I advocate violence against women. I only advocate it against assholes who get your child taken away and turn the world against you by claiming you're a baby thief.

"Larry sounds like he knows his stuff," says Coach.

"How'd you get involved?" I ask him.

"Your teammates bombarded me with texts.

They know the rumors were bullshit." Coach looks at Hector. "Excuse the language, padre."

"I'm not a padre. But no problem," says Hector.

Coach continues answering my question, "I called you, then Mike and Igor, but couldn't reach anyone, so I tried the Grape Ranch. I figured someone would know how to get a hold of you. Hector got on the horn and told me he was already working on a plan."

"I'm, uh, speechless." I run both hands through my hair. "I really don't know what I'd do if you guys hadn't showed up. That detective looked like he was about to drag me off to prison."

"He was just doing his job," says Hector. "He would have eventually gotten to the truth."

"I wish I knew what that is." It never crossed my mind that Fia wasn't mine. Okay, it did, so let me rephrase. I considered that Marli might've slept with some other guy and gotten pregnant. It never crossed my mind that Fia wasn't Marli's. I never considered that the baby was "borrowed" and given to me for safekeeping. But now that I've heard this theory, I can't stop thinking about it. Especially because I've been questioning Marli's sanity all along.

Lara takes my hand and gives it a squeeze. "We're going to figure this out, Dean. I promise."

Heat surges up my arm and swirls around my heart. I beam into Lara's warm brown eyes and suddenly have the urge to kiss her again.

Last we spoke, she wasn't happy with me because Dannie showed up at my apartment, and I didn't hold back the drool. I acted like an immature jerk who thinks with his cock. She had every right to knock me down a few pegs. But the fact that she's here by my side means everything. She didn't turn away, run, tell me to cover my ass and ditch the baby. She put her anger aside for me. For Fia.

And suddenly it clicks.

That impenetrable ten-inch-thick coating around my heart, made up of scar tissue, melts away.

I've always believed that love is man's greatest liability. His ball and chain, holding him back from his dreams. Just like my love for Flip has always been a boat anchor.

But right now, seeing Lara and how she doesn't want or need anything from me—not even an apology for how shitty I behaved—it lights something up. For once, I'm not trying to convince myself that love is a waste of time. I'm telling myself how lucky I'd be to have it. From her.

"I guess the two of us'll be going." Hector claps me on the shoulder, jarring me from my trance.

Coach looks at Hector. "I think he's got it bad," Coach says. "Kinda reminds me of when I met Jo, my wife. I couldn't eat for three months while we dated."

Hector chuckles as the two walk away discussing the matter.

I look at Lara, examining the fine details of her face—the heart-shaped lips, the wide hopeful eyes, the long lashes. I can't find one thing about her I don't like. "You're really beautiful. You know that?"

"Are you saying that because I brought the rescue posse in the nick of time to prevent you from being ass-rape-candy for some guy named Bubba in prison?"

Ew. "Maybe?"

"Thought so." She smiles brightly. "I know it's not over, Dean, but it will be soon. It's going to work out for you. I promise. Call if you need anything." She starts walking away.

"Wait. Don't go."

She stops but doesn't say anything. She looks bothered all of a sudden—frown, tight lips, a sadness in her eyes.

"Lara, I'm really sorry about what happened yesterday. I know sometimes I'm a little…easily distracted. But I can only think of one woman I would actually gouge out my eyes for." *That came out all wrong.* I wanted to say I would never look at another woman if I had her. My thoughts shock me, but they're true.

Lara's mouth contorts with disgust. "Are you trying to be romantic right now?"

"Didn't work, huh?"

"Not even a little. But what's going on here, Dean? What are you trying to say right now?"

Her tone is serious, and I'm not sure if she's

receptive, confused, or stunned. I decide to put a few of my cards on the table and see where it goes.

"I like you," I lie. It's more than that, and I know it.

"I like you, too, Dean. But I'm not sure what that means to you."

She's going to make me say it, isn't she? She wants to know if I'm serious.

"I've never felt anything for anyone," I admit. "So can't we just start there and see where this goes? Take it slow? I mean, look at what's happening. I'm not exactly in a position to start a serious relationship. My life, my future, my everything is balanced on a razor-sharp edge."

I watch the twinkle of hope die in her eyes. "You know what's funny, Dean? Most people say times like these give them razor-sharp clarity. Not razor-sharp blurriness with a side of 'let's keep our options open.'"

Lara turns toward her car, and fuck me, but I really don't want her to go. This moment might be a baby step for most guys—to actually feel something real for a woman—but for me, this is Everest.

Maybe I need to tell her that, but something about this situation feels off, like Lara is purposefully making it too hard. What girl asks for a serious commitment right out of the friendship gate?

It doesn't fit her.

I rush over and block her from her car. "Just tell me why you're pushing me away every chance you get? Because I know you're not weak or afraid or fragile. But every time I make a tiny mistake, you're storming off. Why?"

She looks away. "I can't do this here."

"Okay. Then where?"

"My place."

"I can't. Fia is supposed to be dropped off at my apartment." The detective didn't give me an exact time, so I should stick around at home and wait for the call from Child Services. And yes, I hate that I'll have to see Mike, but it is what it is. I can't change the situation. Not today. Tomorrow is another story.

"I can't go to your place," she says.

"Why? What's the big deal?" I push.

Lara mutters, "Because I can't see Fia right now."

Huh? I feel like I'm falling down a rabbit hole here. Is Lara like Nina? Or Mike? She thinks Fia is toxic to my life?

"Why?"

She refuses to answer.

"Okay. I'll just put you in touch with all the other people who think I'm crazy for caring about a little girl who needs me."

"No." She squeezes her eyes shut like she's in pain. "I adore Fia."

"Then?"

Her gaze locks on the patch of asphalt between our feet. "She looks just like my daughter."

"You have a daughter?"

"Did." Lara's eyes start to overflow with tears as she speaks softly. "I was eighteen when I had her. My family made me give her up." Lara drags a fist under her eyes. "They said I couldn't do it on my own, and they wouldn't help me either. They told me all the reasons she'd be better off without me, with parents who could give her everything she needed." Lara shrugs. "So I gave her up after a month. I signed away all my rights, and since then I've spent every day wishing I'd kept her. I wish…" She inhales sharply and exhales. "That someone, anyone, would have stepped up to help me, to tell me I could figure it all out."

All of my questions about Lara are answered with one quiet confession. And now, more than ever, I respect how incredibly strong she is. The entire time, she's been putting on a brave face around Fia. All to help me.

I bob my head, letting the brutal reality of her situation sink in. "For what it's worth, I think you were brave to let your daughter go. You wanted to give her a better life."

Lara's tears flow in constant streams down her cheeks. "But it was the wrong choice."

I want to hold her, comfort her, but I'm not sure I should. I don't know shit about being there for people. Not like this.

"Lara, you have no idea how things would have worked out if you'd kept her. Life isn't always kind or easy." Honestly, I sometimes wish my mother would have put Flip and me up for adoption. At least then we would have had a chance at growing up with families.

"If it wasn't a mistake, then why've I've spent all these years missing her?"

"Because you're a good person. You care about her. But there is no reason to believe your daughter is miserable or suffering. Who knows, maybe she'll come looking for you someday, and you two will reconnect."

"That's not what I want, Dean. I miss my baby. I want to see her. I want to watch her grow. I want to watch her discover who she's meant to be. I want to watch her fall in love, fall down, and get back up again. I want to bake her birthday cakes and take her shopping. I just..." Lara shakes her head, "want to be a part of her life."

"Never in a million years could I imagine myself saying this, but I understand. I really understand. And for what it's worth, I'm here for you." I wish I could do more, but it's the only thing I have to offer.

CHAPTER SEVENTEEN

Lara insists on coming back to my place to keep me company while I wait for Child Services to call and bring back Fia. The gesture leaves me feeling uneasy. Too many things were left unsaid back at the police station parking lot, and I need to get them off my chest.

For example, I've only had my little dumplin' for a handful of days, so I can't imagine how a woman feels carrying a baby, giving birth, and loving it only to lose it. What I'm getting at is that Lara sees her lost daughter in Fia, but it didn't stop her from helping me. I think it's the kindest thing anyone's ever done.

But where does that leave us?

I'm attracted to Lara physically, something I always knew, but now my eyes have been opened to the quality of person she really is. I want her. Yet this is still the worst possible time to embark on a serious relationship.

And suddenly I'm adding to the list of things I don't care about. I don't care if I have no plan for taking custody of Fia. I don't care if this is a bad time to make a commitment to Lara. I'm flying blind, following my gut. A first for me.

I've got to tell Lara how I feel. Because nothing like this has ever happened and, fuck, if I'm not spinning another plate I don't want to drop.

I park my truck in the back of the complex again because the swarm of reporters out front has tripled. I haven't bothered looking at my phone because there's no point in seeing what people are saying. Can't be good.

I'm going to stick to my plan, listen to the lawyer, and lean on the people I trust. All this will shake out. Or it won't.

When I get to the third floor, I'm greeted by a crowd of reporters lurking in front of my door.

Wonderful. Looks like they've abandoned any and all concerns over trespassing. I'm going to call the police. Or maybe not? The cops aren't exactly on my side right now.

This is some bullshit. I bet Lara, who left a few minutes before me, took one look at these vultures and headed home. That sucks because I really need to finish the conversation we started. I need a plan for how to deal with the "us situation."

"No comment," I say and push past the field of dildos (reporters) to make my way to my front door, slamming it shut behind me.

"You okay?" Lara's sweet voice rings out from inside my apartment.

A wave of relief rolls through me. "I've never been happier to see anyone."

"You just saw me twenty minutes ago."

"Yeah, well, a lot can happen in twenty minutes."

"Like?" she asks.

I'm about to say how much I need her, how during the drive over, I had an epiphany. But I chicken out. *What a guy.* "Are Igor and Mike here?"

"They were leaving when I got here. They said they were going to stay with friends for a few days until the hyenas leave."

For the best. I don't know if Igor feels the same way Mike does, but I don't give a fuck. I don't need more bullshit right now.

"You hungry?" I say, going to my all-brown kitchen. "I can fix us some sandwiches, or I think I have a frozen pizza."

Lara stands in the kitchen doorway. "No, thanks. I'm not hungry. But, hey, are you going to practice tonight?"

Coach and I didn't talk about it, but I'm one hundred percent sure he knows I'm not coming since I'll be here waiting to get Fia back. "No. Why?"

Her eyes dart away.

I hope she doesn't think I let her come over so she could watch the baby. After her confession, I couldn't do that. But my biggest worry now is like I said: where does it leave us?

Suddenly, I'm feeling like one of those idiot guys in those romance movies. My insides are all twisted up.

"I wasn't going to ask you to take care of Fia," I say, "if that's what you're worried about. I heard what you said and—"

"I'm here. I'm trying to deal with my demons. That's all I really know right now."

I lean against the counter and gaze into her eyes. "It means a lot to me."

"It's not what I promised you—full support— and it really bothers me."

"Are you kidding, Lara? You think you haven't done enough?"

"I'm afraid I won't be able to handle being there when you really need me—at that pivotal moment when you're questioning keeping Fia or letting her go."

"I need you now, and you're here. I'm good with that."

"Need?" She blinks.

I step toward her, knowing perfectly well how incredibly uncomfortable all this feels. For me and for her. But I want this more than I want comfortable.

"Want," I say, placing my hands on her waist. "And if you just fought through that swarm of human vultures outside, then I'm hoping you want me back. As more than your friend. Fully committed."

I wait as she stares up into my eyes.

"Well?" I say, my lips thirsting to kiss her.

"Can I be honest?"

Only if you're about to say we should get naked. "Of course."

"No." She takes a small step back.

I'm confused. "I thought this is what you wanted." In the parking lot earlier, she pushed back when I made that comment about my thoughts being balanced on a razor-sharp edge. Then she told me about her baby and the pain she's been going through just to help me out. Why would I want to let a woman like her go?

"Let me rephrase," she says. "I don't believe you really want me. I think your life has just been turned on its head, and what you're really feeling is fear. You need me as a crutch."

"Don't tell me how I feel or what I think, Lara." For example, right now I'm pretty damned sure she's crazy! Because she's hot. She's smart. She's loyal. There's insane chemistry—at least on my part. So why wouldn't I want her?

She sighs, clearly frustrated. "Then explain why, just twenty minutes ago, you said we should see where things go? If you were really into me, Dean, really truly interested, you would have been pushing for something to happen between us." She throws her hands in the air. "Fuck, Dean! I've flirted with you every day the entire summer. You were polite but wouldn't give me the time of day. These last few days, I've been here for you, and—not that I expected anything in return—all I've gotten is a slightly warmer version of you. Suddenly, after I tell you about my daughter, of the pain I've struggled with just to support you, now you want a relationship. Tell me that's not messed up, Dean. Tell me it's not about you waking up and seeing I'm the steady rock you need during the worst storm of your life."

I frown. "Yes, your confession made me see you differently. But this is not about that."

She folds her arms over her chest. "You changed what you wanted in less than twenty minutes. Twenty. You went from 'let's keep this casual' to 'let's be a couple.'"

"I've always been attracted to you," I say. "Albeit right now I'm questioning that." For the first damned time in my life, I've let myself want a woman. Really want her. I was ready to tear my damned chest open and hand over my heart. *And this is how she responds?*

"Nice, Dean," she snaps, her chest rising and falling rapidly with seething breaths.

"No. You're...*nice*," I throw back because, apparently, I've decided to behave like a first grader in response to her rejection. "And you want to know what else is nice? That I don't want to be in a relationship right now. I don't have the time or the energy to add more plates to my table. But I was willing to try. For you."

She presses her hands over her heart. "Wow. Thank you, Mr. *No*-Land. Thank you for gracing me with your epic love charity. Lucky, lucky me that the great Hot Daddy Dean would make such a sacrifice to take me as his girl."

Damn. I guess what I said did come out a little douchey.

Lara turns to leave.

"Where are you going? The reporters are out there."

"I'd rather face them than listen to your BS." She opens the front door, and the apartment floods with the sound of yelling reporters for a short moment before the door slams shut.

"Fine! I have better things to do anyway!" I march to my kitchen and grab a cold one from the fridge. I pop off the top, take a swig, and set it on the counter. The frosty fizz does nothing to calm the fire in my chest.

How dare she! I don't want a relationship because I feel needy or insecure. I've been on my own most of my life. I know how to handle bad, bad, horrible things, like hunger or having no electricity because my uncle spent his money on whisky and coke. I know what it's like to lie to every adult I met from the age of ten straight through to eighteen, telling them my mom was at work or that the rent would be paid if they'd just give us a few more days. I'm damned good at survival. I perform my best when faced with adversity.

I know how to…

The feeling in my chest starts to tighten. It's the pedestal complex. Only this time, I'm the one putting myself up there. Gotta love it.

I go to my living room and sit on the couch, spearing my fingers through my hair. "God, I'm so messed up."

My phone vibrates in my pocket. I dig it out, hopeful it's someone telling me that Fia is on the way. "Hello?"

"Dean, it's me. Marli."

CHAPTER EIGHTEEN
LARA

I get to my car and lock the doors. These stupid reporters are like horseflies, buzzing all around me. I can't leave unless I run someone over.

Idiots. As if I'm going to make a statement telling them that Dean is part of a baby-trafficking ring. Who'd believe that anyway? Of course, these days, the news is willing to jump on any story they hear. Doesn't matter if it's true. Just as long as someone—anyone—posts it on Twitter.

Bigfoot! Caught on tape buying underwear at Neiman Marcus! Boxers or briefs? You won't believe the answer.

New discovery! The Earth really is flat. See photos NASA has hidden for four hundred years.

This just in. Poll shows that politicians are the most trusted people in America.

After a few minutes, the flies realize they'll have to feed their hunger for fake bullcrap elsewhere. I'm about to head back to my place when I'm overwhelmed with the urge to stay.

The thing is, I want Dean, but that was never in question. The problem has always been that he didn't want me back. At least, not the way I needed. Maybe he flirted a little once. Super casual. Unfortunately, I'm not a casual person. I don't sleep with, give myself to, or share my life with anyone who's not worth my time. I learned my lesson the hard way when the people I loved and trusted most in this world turned their backs and made me give up my baby.

Fine. Okay. *I* gave her up. It was *my* choice. But I'd been convinced I'd be hurting her if I didn't put her up for adoption. Wanting her was selfish, they said.

Now I know the truth. My parents just didn't want the inconvenience. They had their life plan: retire early, travel, do whatever they wanted when they wanted. My own mother said that being a grandmother at forty-one wasn't her plan, so I had to deal with "the problem."

I was just out of high school and had delayed starting college, even though I'd been accepted to a great university. My parents convinced me that my future was ahead of me, but only if I gave up the baby. Otherwise, my life would be one of struggle and poverty. They made it clear they would not support me in any way since it was "my mistake," not theirs.

Of course, raising a child on my own terrified me, so that was that. I gave her up and went on with my life—college, career, a dream of running my own winery someday.

But I live every day with the choice I made, and while I want to move on, I know a part of me never will. I allowed the people around me to influence the biggest decision of my life. I trusted them. And they abused that trust by putting themselves first.

The point is, trust is everything to me, and I don't trust Dean. Not that I think he's bad or a liar. He just doesn't know what he wants yet. His life has been turned on its head, and he's treading pretty rough waters.

But here's the thing: I would put myself through emotional hell if I knew he was serious about me. I would find a way to get through the stabbing pain in my heart to be with him and Fia. They'd be worth it. I'm just not going to put myself through that if Dean only wants a fling.

I probably need to tell him all this. He probably thinks I'm walking away because I can't handle being around Fia. He doesn't know I'm willing to try to figure this out.

I'm about to go back out into shark-infested waters and return to Dean's apartment when I spot him shimmying down his balcony's railing.

"What the…?"

I observe him swing like a large monkey and land feetfirst in his downstairs neighbor's balcony.

What is he doing? He's a huge guy, and those railings do not look—

Dean swings one leg over the next railing and then gets his second leg over.

"Oh God." I cover my mouth, watching him maneuver down the wobbly barrier. "Dean, that's not going to hold your—"

An entire section of the old iron railing comes loose, and Dean hurtles to the ground, landing on a hedge. He bounces and tumbles face-first onto the sidewalk that skirts around the building.

"Oh shit!" I'm about to get out of my car and run to him, but he hops to his feet like a cat and sprints off to his truck.

Where is he going? Somewhere he doesn't want the press to follow.

I crank my engine, wait a few seconds, and tail him.

⪼ ⪻

DEAN

Child Services is supposed to call and then drop off Fia at my place soon, so I don't have much time, but I have to do this. Marli says she's just down the road at a motel.

"Don't let anyone follow you, Dean. I mean it," she said. "This is life or death."

"What's wrong?" I asked.

"I'll tell you when you get here. I'm in room one-twenty."

I want answers, so I didn't argue. Especially not

now. People think Fia is stolen, and Marli is the only person who can set the record straight.

I make a few laps around the neighborhood to ensure no one's following. I think I'm good, so I continue to the Ultra Mega Love Motel. Let's just say it's the sort of place that rents rooms by the hour.

I park in back, so my truck isn't visible from the road, and find the room around the front. My heart is pounding in my chest. I'm angry. I'm worried. I'm praying that Marli is going to confirm Fia is mine.

What if she's here to take Fia? I think.

Crap. It didn't cross my mind until now. If she is mine, I'll need to do that paternity test tomorrow morning as planned. It's my only chance of being part of Fia's life.

I knock, and the door opens. Marli is standing there looking very different from the last and only time I saw her. Her blonde hair is a stringy mess. She has dark circles under her green eyes. Her clothes are wrinkled and dirty.

"Hurry. Come in." She steps aside, and I enter, closing the door behind me. I'm on pins and needles.

"What's going on?"

Marli hugs her stomach with shaky arms. "I lied to you."

"So it's true. Fia isn't mine."

She shakes her head. "I don't know, Dean. I'm

sorry, but I just don't know." She walks over to sit on the bed, which is covered in a dark, ugly floral bedspread. Probably to hide the stains. "I slept with my husband a few days after I met you."

I'm furious. "So why lie to me? Do you have any fucking idea what I'm going through? The world thinks I stole her. My career is probably over. You have to come with me to the police station and set the record—"

"My husband is Tony 'the rolling pin' Rigatoni."

"What the shit?" I know exactly who he is. For starters, it's a ridiculous name. Also, it's kind of hard to forget a guy who murders someone by beating him to death with a rolling pin. I think Tony got off on some technicality. Either way, the internet is full of conspiracy theories about him having ties to powerful government officials, and he has a pretty large meme following. Kind of an Angry Cat meets Bernie Sanders mittens situation.

Marli goes on, "When you and I met, I couldn't tell you the truth about who I really am. I definitely couldn't say I was on the run from Tony."

"It was a much better decision to hide the fact your husband is a murderous criminal," I say sarcastically.

"You have no idea how murderous." She shakes her head.

"Then why go back to him?" I ask.

"I didn't. Some friend of his spotted me at a gas

station. Completely random." She whooshes out a breath. "The guy tailed me, and when Tony caught up, I had to pretend I was just trying to punish him because I saw him with another woman a few weeks earlier. I told him I planned to come back after he suffered for a while, but in truth, I'd been planning my escape for months."

"Why were you with him in the first place?"

She throws her arms to her sides. "He always denied he was anything more than an accountant. He made me believe that his clients just *happened* to be Italians who were being unjustly persecuted by the feds over their nationality." Her eyes fill with fear. "I found out the truth eventually. He's dangerous. He's killed at least fifty or sixty people if I'm going by his kitchen utensil collection."

"What?"

"He likes to cook, so he buys himself a new utensil every time he murders someone. It's his thing."

Okay. She's married to a psychopathic, murdering accountant who enjoys collecting spatulas and stuff, which in itself is a telltale sign that something is the matter with the guy. "I'm guessing he's after you now and wants Fia back?"

"He doesn't know about her."

Phew! "Does he know about me?"

"No."

Double phew!

She continues, "After he caught up with me the

last time, I stayed for a month until I realized I was pregnant. I've been on the run ever since. I had Fia in an ER and ran with her before any public record could be made."

"So you have zero documents to prove she's yours." *And…I'm back to square one. Awesome.*

"No, but I have much bigger problems, Dean. My sister passed away last week, and I had to go to the funeral. I knew it would be a risk because Tony might be looking for me there, but I couldn't miss it. She was everything to me—my best friend."

So that's why she needed to leave the baby with me. Marli was willing to risk her own life but wasn't willing to risk Tony finding out about Fia. I want to say it was a stupid choice to go to the funeral, but I'd probably do the same if it were Flip. Lately, things have been crazy, but I usually see or talk to him on the phone once a week. We're close.

"So you didn't want to risk Tony finding out about Fia." I bob my head, trying to let it all sink in.

"He can't ever know about her, Dean. Not ever. If he does, he won't rest until he has her. He's possessive about his things, and he'll see her as one of them. He'll kill anyone who gets in his way."

And awesome again. How did I get so lucky? "But what if she's not his? What if she's mine?"

"It doesn't matter."

"It matters to me."

"That's not what I meant. If he finds out I had her, and it's documented she's yours, he'll know I cheated. He'll kill you, Dean. He'll kill your family, your friends, your pets, your houseplant, your dishwasher, your—"

"Okay. I get it. He'll kill. A lot."

"Once he's done with you, he'll come for me, too. But he won't kill me. He'll make me pay first. Toes, fingers, lips, ears, teeth—"

"Okay. I get it." Basically, if Fia is connected to Marli in any way, someone dies.

I'm strangely relieved to finally know the truth. Yet I also have the sudden urge to dye my hair, grow a really big mustache, and move somewhere no one wants to live. Maybe San Francisco would work. Too much human poop on the sidewalks.

"I'm so sorry, Dean. I never meant for this to happen." The sadness in her eyes tugs on my heartstrings.

"So what's your plan?" I sit on the bed next to her.

"To disappear. For good. I just want to see her one last time."

I want to swear. I want to yell at this woman I hardly know, but I can't bring myself to do it. She's been through some pretty bad stuff. "I don't know what to say. Your plan leaves me out on a ledge, because I won't be able to prove Fia's mine."

"Exactly. You can't ever have her blood tested, Dean. Not even at a private lab. Tony is smart. He has connections everywhere. And I'm one hundred percent sure he's using them to try to find me. They probably have my DNA flagged in the FBI database—Fia has my DNA."

"Why would your DNA be flagged?"

She shrugs. "In case my body turns up somewhere, he'll know."

"That's grim."

"It's reality. And it's why I came to warn you. Once I saw what people were saying in the news, I worried you might try to prove she's your daughter."

"Only because I don't want them to take her."

Marli gives me a serious look. "You should let them."

"Wait. You never planned to come back, did you?" I conclude. "You hoped I'd hand her over to Child Services." She said she'd done her research, so that means she knew my situation. College student. Scholarship. Budding football career.

"Don't be mad. I needed to make sure she had a chance." She covers her hand with mine and squeezes.

"Then why not dump her at some orphanage? Leave her with Child Services yourself? Why put me through all this?"

"I tried a thousand times—I swear I did—but then I'd drive away with her."

"Then why not keep her, Marli?"

"Because, Dean! He *will* find me! And then what?"

I'm beginning to see her predicament, and I

can't say I'd do anything differently.

I exhale with a frustrated groan. "What am I going to do?"

"Make sure she finds a good home and then get as far away from her as possible—for her own good."

My heart falls into an instant rage. "You said she might be mine."

"What's it matter if you're dead, Dean? Because you can't prove a thing—not without risking tipping off Tony."

"You can't do this to me. If Fia is my daughter, I don't want to lose her." I can't even say I wouldn't want her even if she had the blood of a coldhearted killer with an obsession for baking paraphernalia.

"If you love her even a fraction as much as I do, then she's all that matters. You have to do what you can to protect her. And right now, this is as good as it gets; Tony doesn't know she exists, and he'll never find out if you let her go. Just be sure to tell the police whatever they need to hear so no one doubts your story and tests her DNA. Get them to believe I am just a nobody who abandoned her baby."

"This is crazy. I need to think." I need a tranquilizer, too.

"I understand, Dean. But please don't take too long. I was careful not to be seen at my sister's funeral, but I'm worried."

"Why?" I ask.

"Because I didn't spot Tony or any of his

henchmen lurking."

"Maybe he gave up on you." Marli could be paranoid.

"It means they did a better job of hiding than me," she says.

"Did they follow you here?"

"I took precautions, but in this day and age, it doesn't take long to track down a person. Every bridge, toll road, and intersection has cameras. It's only a matter of time before they find footage of me driving away from the funeral. Once they have that, they'll know the car I'm in and find me. I don't have much time. A day at best."

"Wonderful."

She adds, "I'll call you tomorrow morning at exactly six forty-three. If I do, then meet me at Liberty Park at noon. I'll be wearing a red baseball cap. If I don't call you at that time, don't go. And if I'm wearing any other color hat, drive away."

I wonder if her hat collection includes one that's made of aluminum foil. She sounds completely paranoid. Not that Tony isn't dangerous, but she's making it seem like he's got the CIA after her or something. "Marli, come on…"

"I'm serious, Dean."

"Let's go to the police. We can figure something out—"

"If I could trust those people, I would. But Tony has too many connections. I don't want you or Fia getting mixed up in any of this. Got it?"

"But she's your kid. You can't just walk awa—"

"I can, Dean. Because I love her that much. And so should you."

I rub my forehead. "I don't know."

"You don't have to know. You just have to do what's right."

CHAPTER NINETEEN

I walk to my truck, my head spinning like a tornado of emotions. I almost wish I didn't know the truth about Marli and her husband because now I'll never be free of it. *Or be able to look at a kitchen utensil the same way.*

I unlock my door and slide behind the wheel. I know if I give the situation enough thought, I'll figure out a way to fix it, because what Marli is suggesting is a lose-lose for everyone. She never gets to see Fia again and lives on the run. Her husband roams free, always a threat to us all. I lose my football career because without a very public, well-documented rebuttal to the claims being made about Fia, I'll always be seen as a baby snatcher.

I wish I could have Mr. Rolling Pin give that Dannie woman a baking lesson. This is just as much her fault as Tony's. I still don't know why she started all this on social media.

The passenger door of my truck flies open, and Lara hops in, making me jump in my seat.

"Jesus, woman. What are you doing here?"

"I followed you. You suck at shaking people, by the way. And don't you Jesus woman me, Dean!" She points an angry finger in my face. "I can't believe you. I can't believe after everything you said an hour ago, you're coming here and hooking up for paid sex!"

"But I—"

"No, Dean. No more lies." She throws her arms in the air. "And to think I was going to tell you I'm in love with you, that I would find a way to work through my feelings about my daughter just to be a part of your life. And here you are, poking the paid pussy!"

Yikes. Who says that? And... "What's the matter with you? I am not here for..." My voice fades. I can't tell her the real reason I'm here. I can't drag her into this.

I swallow a bitter lump in my throat. "Yes, I admit it. I was poking the paid pussy. And I'm very sorry." I shrug. "I guess I just really, really needed some womanly affection." I feel like a moron. Also, I need to make it sound more believable. That was pretty damned pathetic. "I needed to pound one out. Hard. Like a man does." That came out even worse.

Lara narrows her eyes. "What are you up to?"

"Nothing. Other than that thing you just caught me doing."

"Nuh-uh. You're lying. I can tell."

Why does she have to be so smart? It's annoying. "Believe me or don't believe me. But I—"

My cell rings, and I frantically dig it out of my jeans pocket, hoping it's Child Services. "Hello?"

It's a Ms. Blackwell, Fia's caseworker, confirming that she has Fia and is on the way to my apartment. I confirm my address and agree to meet her in twenty minutes.

I end the call and look at Lara. "I have to go. They're dropping off Fia."

"You do what you have to." Lara hops out and beelines toward the front side of the motel.

I exit my truck. "Dammit, Lara! Where are you going? I need to get back to my place."

"I'm going to find out what you're hiding," she yells.

I scrub my face with my hands and groan. I have to leave, but I can't let Lara get mixed up in this.

I chase after Lara, who's now disappeared around the corner. I swear I'm going to throttle her for this.

I turn the corner, and *oomph!* I collide with some guy's shoulders, and it nearly sends me to the ground.

"Hey! Watch where you're going, buddy," the guy says. He's dressed in a black Members Only jacket and black slacks. His dark brown hair is covered with a baseball cap.

"Why don't you..." *Oh fuck.* I know his face. It's Tony. "Why don't you have a nice night, sir.

And very sorry about that." I keep walking, my heart racing a million miles a second.

No, no, no. If he's here, and he's leaving…

I bolt toward Marli's room just in time to see Lara running away from it, in the opposite direction. I can't see Lara's face, but I can tell something's wrong.

"Lara!" I call out but keep heading to Marli's room. When I get to the doorway, all I see is her body lying on the floor, a ladle sticking out of her bloody mouth.

What the…? She's dead.

Every muscle in my body floods with anger. And fear. And more anger. Tony Rigatoni did this.

I stand there, unable to think straight or wrap my head around what I'm looking at. I was just with Marli. I *just* talked to her.

She can't be dead. I glance inside the room again. *Yep. She's dead.* I don't know if I should call the police or go to the manager or what. Lara will know what to do.

I turn my head in the direction she went, only to see Lara is peeling rubber out of there.

"Wait!" I dig my cell from my pocket and call her, but my call goes to voicemail.

If she saw what I saw, Lara is upset. She probably needs me. But I have to get home for Fia. I have to put the baby first.

❧ ❧

I'm going to be sick. When I get back to my place, I'm a sweaty, shaky mess. I grew up in a rough neighborhood, so that wasn't my first time seeing a dead body, but I've never witnessed anyone murdered in that particular way. Also, there's the fact that I knew her. She was Fia's mother.

This is a nightmare. I grip my steering wheel, thinking about how it all happened so fast. If I'd left Marli's motel room a minute later, I probably would have been right beside her with an ice cream scoop or a pair of salad tongs shoved in my face.

What am I going to tell Fia if she asks about her mother? It's actually a moot point, because Marli was right; I need to make sure Fia is never discovered. If she fell into Tony's hands, God only knows what he'd do the first time she upsets him. Fia can never know about Tony or Marli either.

I try Lara's cell again and leave her a voicemail warning her not to call the police. Then I text her: *If you say anything, you'll regret it. So don't.*

I park my truck and go around to the back stairwell of my apartment complex. There are still two vulture-mobiles parked out front, so I'm prepared to fight them off.

I jog up the stairs and am greeted by an aggressive reporter with an iPhone she points in my face. "Why are you sneaking out of your apartment, Mr. Norland? What do you have to hide? How many babies have you trafficked?"

"You're all idiots. Go home," I tell her. "Or better yet, try reporting some real news for once. If that's too difficult, I hear a unicorn just stabbed a vampire down at the Quickmart."

They ignore me and start yelling questions about where I got Fia.

Losers. I go for my keys, but the door's unlocked. Maybe one of my roomies came home. I step inside and slam the door behind me.

"Mr. Norland, there you are." An older woman with a lavender dye job is sitting in my living room, holding Fia.

All my worries instantly take a back seat when I lay eyes on the tiny little baby sleeping in her arms. I can't wait to hold her and feel that rush of serenity wash through me.

"How did you get in?" I ask the woman, who has an official-looking lanyard around her neck that includes her photo. She must be Blackwell, the woman who called from Child Services.

"Your friend." Blackwell's eyes move across the room to Lara, who's standing there looking upset— pale face, nauseated expression.

"Lara, I wasn't expecting you to be here." And she got here fast. Must've driven straight over. *But why not answer my calls?*

I don't like this. Something feels off. I mean, more off. This entire evening is an exercise in offness. *And being offed. Poor Marli.*

"I arrived a minute ago and found Ms. Blackwell knocking on your door. I let her in."

"Actually, Mr. Norland," says Ms. Blackwell, looking down her nose at me, "the door was unlocked. Do you make it a habit of doing that? It's very unsafe."

I must've forgotten since I snuck out the balcony. Got a twig up my ass and nearly broke my damned neck, too. "Oh. Uh, no. It's just been a crazy day with all the reporters out there."

She eyes me like I'm a bag of trash she wants to toss to the curb. "Your friend here was just about to tell me something she feels concerned about, weren't you?" Blackwell looks at Lara.

Oh no. What is she doing? My pulse races. "Lara, can I speak to you for a sec?"

"I think I'd rather stay right here." Lara's tone is cold. "Away from any ladles."

A lightbulb goes on. I think I know why she raced to beat me here. She thinks I killed Marli. She's here to protect Fia. *That's really sweet.* Also, really bad.

"But you don't think…?" I point to my chest. "You're not insinuating that…? Lara, what you saw wasn't—I didn't—how could you think that?"

"You murdered," Lara sees my pleading, terrified expression and switches gears, "my love for you. You have some explaining to do."

Phew. She's giving me the benefit of the doubt.

Blackwell's face contorts. "Mr. Norland? What's going on?"

"I *promise* it's a misunderstanding," I say stiffly,

looking right at Lara.

"I saw it with my own eyes, Dean," Lara replies.

So she *does* think I killed Marli. She also believes Marli is some hooker I just banged in a cheap motel. *Bang 'em and kill 'em. Totally my thing.* I'm more than insulted that Lara believes I'm capable of doing something that horrific. "You're going to have to trust me when I say I would never do anything like that."

Blackwell frowns, looking thoroughly confused.

"What about that text you sent?" Lara asks. "Sounded like you were offering to use your utensils on me."

"No. I was trying to say that certain people—not me—are very picky about how their utensils are used and wouldn't appreciate you...rating them." That came out all wrong. I wanted to say that Tony Rigatoni is a man she doesn't want to cross.

"Is this some sort of sex talk code?" Blackwell asks.

"You caught us," I say. "Sorry. Lara and I are a new couple, and we had a fight over...the wedding registry gifts. This is our form of makeup sex. Verbal banter."

Blackwell's wrinkled lips twist sideways. "But you just said you're a new couple."

"Yes. Yes, I did." *I need to stop talking now.* "Yet," I walk over to Lara and throw my arm around her, "I know she's the one. So why wait?"

Blackwell bobs her head slowly. She either

thinks we're on something or we're stupid. "All right, well, I have to get home to my cats, so I need you to show me around the apartment. Then I'll schedule a follow-up visit with you for next week."

"Follow-up?" I ask.

"Standard procedure."

I'm not about to argue with the woman. I just want her to leave. Then I need to figure out what to tell Lara. She's going to freak the hell out.

"Sure. I'd be happy to show you around." I gesture toward my bedroom.

Blackwell rises from the couch, still holding a sleeping Fia. I try not to think about what just happened to her mother. It's sad. It's disturbing. It's driven home the danger I'm facing. *We're* facing.

After an embarrassing tour of my place that included showing off Mike's mountain of dirty underwear on his floor and Igor's stack of Eastern European porn magazines, Blackwell gives me a pile of paperwork to sign, releasing Fia back into my care.

"I feel like I'm buying a car," I say.

She doesn't laugh at my joke. Meanwhile, Lara is still eyeing me with extreme suspicion.

"I'll call you to schedule that visit next week, Mr. Norland." Blackwell hands Fia over, and I melt with relief. I've missed my little squishy football. "Looking forward to it."

I show Blackwell out and lock the door. When I turn around, Lara is holding a meat tenderizer in one hand and her cell in the other. "I'm going to give you sixty seconds to explain what happened back at that motel, or I'm calling 911. And it'd better be the truth, Dean. The entire truth."

I figured I'd have to tell her some of the facts, but tell her everything? I'm not so sure that's a good idea. "I can't, Lara. And it's not because I've done anything wrong. It's because I don't want you dragged into this."

"I'm already dragged."

"You don't understand—"

"I understand that I confessed I'm in love with you tonight, while sitting in the parking lot of a motel used exclusively for meth heads and hookers, and then I found the woman you just had sex with lying on the floor with a ladle sticking out of her face. How you even did that, I can't imagine, but for as long as I live, I will never be able to serve soup like a normal person. I'm probably stuck with using mugs or those serving spoons that take forever to fill your bowl with."

"Did you say you love me?"

Lara's face contorts. "That's the part of this you want to discuss?"

Yes, I do because I completely missed it earlier, and when a woman you're falling for says she loves you, it feels off to just let it fly by unnoticed.

"See," I say, "this is exactly what I was trying to

explain before. It's bad timing for a relationship. I should've reacted when you said you loved me. Instead, I didn't even hear you." She deserves better.

"Back up a sec, Dean, and start with what happened at that motel."

If I tell her, it's going to bring a whole new kind of worry to her life. The Tony Rigatoni kind.

"Hold on," I say, hit with a new thought, "did you see a man leaving that room?"

"No. There was just some guy walking through the parking lot away from it."

Tony. "Did he see you? Did you see his face?"

"Sure. Why?" She shrugs.

"Because now you *are* in it." If Tony thinks she's a witness, will he try to track her down? I have to tell her everything. If I don't, she won't be prepared for the dangerous mess we're in. "Okay. Here goes. But once I tell you, you can't say a word to anyone. If you do, the consequences could cost me everything."

Lara stares for a long moment. "Please don't tell me you're part of a baby-trafficking ring."

"That would be good news compared to this."

CHAPTER TWENTY

LARA

I can't believe what I'm hearing. I mean, Tony "the rolling pin" Rigatoni? He's a notorious mobster type who got away with murder.

And now he's killed again. *With a ladle no less.* The entire situation is a sad, scary mess, including the fact that this makes it impossible for Dean to prove Fia is not stolen.

You poor little girl. I look at Fia, the cutest little baby on the planet, snuggled tightly in Dean's manly and doting arms.

Sigh… He's a natural with his daughter. That is, if she's really his. In my mind, though, what does it matter? Dean can't ever let that baby get into the hands of a violent disturbed criminal.

For fuck's sake, Tony just murdered Fia's mom. I have no clue what's going to happen when she's discovered.

Maybe nothing.

The running joke in town is that the Ultra Mega Love Motel is where people go to die. Kind of like my apartment when it comes to houseplants. Anyway, someone turns up dead there at least once a month. The news hardly reports on it, and if they do, it's buried in the back of the paper. The residents of this town just don't want to hear about it anymore.

"I'm going to put Fia down," Dean says.

"I should get going. It's getting late," I say.

"No. Don't leave."

"I really should—"

"Give me a sec." Dean disappears, but it's more like five minutes before he returns. He's holding two clean juice glasses and a bottle of whiskey. "I think the situation calls for hard alcohol."

"Oh, I shouldn't. I need to drive home."

Dean sits next to me and places the bottle and the glasses on the coffee table. "No, you don't. Mike and Igor are gone. I have the place to myself. You can crash on the couch. Or take my bed. Whichever you like."

"Why?" His beautiful hazel eyes fixate on my lips. My pulse rate accelerates. I want to believe his desire is real, especially now when my emotions are running high. But so are his. He probably needs an outlet.

I know I sure do.

"I want you to stay because I'd feel better knowing you're here. Safe with me."

It's sweet that Dean wants to protect me, but it's not necessary. *Or maybe it is, and I'm in denial.*

"You really think that Tony guy is going to come after me?"

"I don't know what to think anymore. I just need to sleep, and I'll do it much better if I'm not worrying about you."

But he knows how hard it is for me to be here with him and Fia. *It feels like...like...*I press my hand over my heart. "I can't believe it."

"What?"

"I didn't think of her. Not once."

"Who?" Dean stares for a long moment. "Oh. Your daughter."

"Does that make me a bad person?" I wonder out loud. I must be because I should be thinking about that poor dead woman back at the motel. Instead, I'm thinking about my own problems.

Dean slides his big rough hand over mine. "No, it doesn't. And it's time you stop punishing yourself."

The tears start to well in my eyes, but I push them back. He's right. I know he is. "I'm tired of feeling like this all the time."

"Then don't. Forgive yourself."

"I just feel like..." I shake my head. I don't want to say how I feel because I'm sick of that old broken record playing in my head.

"Like you are the smartest, sexiest, most amazing person I've ever met?" Dean stares down at me, his eyes filled with adoration.

My stomach churns, and my heart starts going

crazy. Not because of his words but because of the way he's looking at me. "You really mean it, don't you?"

"Just like I meant it earlier when I said I wanted you."

"I want you, too," I admit. It feels good and weird and uncomfortable to say it, but when I look at this guy, he drives me crazy. I love how he stays strong even when he has doubts. I love how he fights for what's right, even when he stands to lose everything. I love how hot he looks in those tight white pants on the field. Yes, I've seen videos of him playing. Hot.

"But you do understand, Lara, that I can't offer you perfect. It kills me to say it, because out of everything and everyone in my life, you're the one who probably deserves it. You and Fia. And knowing I'm going to struggle just to give you a fraction of what you deserve gets under my skin. I want to give you perfect because you're perfect. To me, anyway."

I blink up at him and slide my hand on his rough cheek. He's let his stubble grow out into a short beard. I'm guessing because he's had other things to worry about. What he doesn't know is that it only makes him look more rugged and sexy. Yes, it's official; everything about this guy makes me swoon, even his lazy grooming. "Your saying that only makes me want to be with you more."

Our eyes lock for a long moment, and I'm praying he's going to kiss me. I need it. I want it.

My prayers are answered, and he leans in. I lean in, too, but go slow, wanting to soak in the moment and remember every second.

Dean wants me, and I want him, and there's nothing casual about the way we feel.

His lips press to mine, gentle at first. I savor the soft texture of his mouth, surrounded by rough whiskers tickling the edges of my lips. I inhale deeply, wanting to immerse myself in his scent, which is oddly sweet.

I suddenly realize he smells like Fia. Sweet baby smell. It's like cotton candy infused with love. It instantly takes me back to memories of holding my daughter. The smell of her hair, the soft little hands, the gentle breaths.

I abruptly pull away from Dean.

"Is something wrong?" he asks.

I bite my lower lip. "I'm, uh—it's going to take some time is all."

"Did I do something wrong?"

"No. Not at all. You just smell like…baby shampoo and…" My voice fades off.

"Ah. I see." Dean exhales softly, offering a comforting smile. "Take all the time you need. Just don't leave. Don't give up on us."

It means a lot that he's willing to let me set the pace. It means he's telling the truth: he does want me. The way he handled that makes him all the more sexy.

"Why don't we get some rest." He holds up his hands. "I can take the couch."

"No. No. You need your bed and a good night's sleep. I'll stay out here."

He nods solemnly and leaves, returning with linens and a pillow. "If you change your mind, come to my room. To sleep. Nothing more." He sets the pile on the edge of the couch.

"Thank you."

He kisses my lips, and I'm back to wanting him again. How long will this yo-yoing last? Forgiving myself won't be easy, but Dean's right. I have to. I have to stop beating myself up for something I can't change.

After an hour of tossing and turning, I throw in the towel. I'd be better off at home in my bed. I'm about to leave, but then I remember Dean asking me to stay as a favor to him. He'll panic if I'm not here when he wakes up. Maybe I need a more comfortable place to sleep.

I tiptoe to his room, which is infused with the smell of his woodsy cologne and Fia's baby lotion. I slide into bed and curl up next to him, placing my head on his chest.

"Glad you came," he grumbles.

I actually didn't, but I'm hoping to. Soon. Being around him is like a shock to my system every time. How's it possible to want a guy so much and not be able to make that step?

DEAN

The next morning, I'm lying in bed, still half asleep, when I realize Lara is next to me, facing away. And there's this second where I've forgotten all the shit happening in my life. Everything is perfect. There's this amazing woman in my bed, who's taking over my heart. Lust has always been there for her, but there's something sexy and delicious about the pace we're taking. There's a desire building in my chest, in my heart, and…*In my shorts.*

Oh fuck. I look under the covers at my morning wood. I turn my head, grateful that Lara is still sleeping.

I slowly slide from the bed and am almost to the doorway when Fia whimpers in her crib. I clench my eyes shut, as if that'll magically stop her from waking up Lara.

But, alas, my only choice is getting to the bathroom quickly and resolving the issue. *Go, go, go.*

"Dean?"

I freeze but don't turn around. Otherwise, Lara'll see my enormous morning salute. "Be right back. Just going to the bathroom."

"Do you have a boner, Dean?" she says teasingly.

"I'm hating you right now." I march to the bathroom, the sound of Lara's giggles fading as I close the door.

Luckily, my issue is resolved with a quick-and-easy emptying of the bladder along with a short visualization sequence involving grandmas in enormous old lady panties and support bras—a trick I learned when I was in my teens and my elderly neighbor's mail came to our apartment by accident. I thought I'd find something exciting in her *Woman's Wear* catalog. Imagine my surprise when I couldn't have an erection for an entire month.

I gargle with mouthwash and return to my room. Lara is still in my bed, and dammit if I don't want her. But I can't go there until she's ready. Also, baby.

"Everything taken care of?" she mutters with her eyes closed.

"Yes. Thank you."

"It's okay, Dean." She cracks open one eye. "I'm a grown woman. I know what happens to men in the morning."

"I'm sure you do, but I'm trying to keep the mystery alive for as long as possible. Because once you see it all, the magic is lost."

"Hilarious." She chuckles. "So how did you sleep?"

I sit beside her on the bed. "Better than ever. Even Fia slept through the night. Maybe it's a sign." I gaze into her soft brown eyes. I want to take things to the next level: naked. So waiting is going to be difficult.

"So what's the plan for today?" she asks with a

strain in her voice. I know she's worried like I am about this Tony guy.

"Good question." I throw my head back and exhale. "I have practice tonight."

"Oh."

"I can ask Coach's wife to help with Fia," I say.

"What happened to your neighbor, that Nina woman?"

"She sees a future for us I don't share—one that doesn't include Fia."

"She actually said that?" Lara asks.

"Pretty much. Also, I want a future with you, so that puts a damper on her evil plot to become my vag-tator."

"What's that?"

"The female version of dictator." I crack a smile. "It's also a food-fetish thing Mike told me about. You don't want to know."

"You're absolutely correct." Lara sits up, and I try not to check her out. Might come off as creepy after my boner incident.

"Well," she continues, "I have to be at the Ranch in forty minutes. Why don't I watch her tonight? I can be back around 4:30."

"You don't have to do that," I say.

"I want to. I think I want to face this head-on. Otherwise, I'm going to keep living in the past."

I can't help beaming at her. Lara's strength is what first attracted me—she's a confident woman— but she's also warm and caring.

"What?" Her cheeks flush.

I brush my hand over her soft cheek. "I could get used to seeing you in my bed." I start to lean in for a kiss. I don't even care if she has morning breath. I'd kiss her even if she'd just eaten a pile of sardines or the world's hottest chili pepper.

"Wah!" Fia's tiny voice pierces my ears.

"And that would be the breakfast bell," I say, stopping two inches shy of her lips.

Lara sighs. "I have to go anyway."

"I know."

I go to pick up Fia, who has the biggest saggy diaper I've ever seen. "Oh, my poor girl. I bet your bootie is cold." I kiss her forehead. "I'm gonna get you all dry and make some of that warm nasty formula for your belly. Yum!"

"Dean?"

"Yeah?" I grab a fresh diaper from my dresser along with the changing pad.

"We still don't have a plan. What happens if the police figure out we were at the motel? What if Tony comes after us? What if he's never implicated? He can't go free again."

I'm the guy who believes in plans and in making them happen, but I don't have the answers.

"I'm not sure what the plan is. Tony saw both our faces, but it was dark, and he took off before we did. If he didn't follow us home, it's going to be hard to track either of us down." Unless the police figure out we were there somehow. That would change everything because our faces and names will be all over the news.

I refrain from telling Lara this because she can probably figure it out on her own. If she hasn't, I don't want her to worry about something that hasn't happened yet. "Just be careful, okay? Any sign of Tony, you call the police."

"I wish I could skip work today and hide out at a friend's house."

"Don't be afraid. Everything's going to work out. Okay?" I'm guessing the police will process Marli's crime scene and get her DNA. Maybe Tony's, too, if he touched the ladle. Either way, it's only a question of time before they find out who she was. Once they do, the first person they'll suspect is Tony—the guy who's a known murderer. "All we have to do is wait it out. The police will figure out who killed Marli."

"If they don't?"

"Then there are two witnesses who'll have to consider stepping forward, but I don't see a reason to do it until we have to." I exhale, feeling relieved.

"Why do you look happy all of a sudden?"

"I don't know. I think because I just came up with a plan and it didn't stress me out." I smile at her. "See, you're good for me."

"We're good for each other." She smiles weakly, trying to be upbeat. Not so easy to do at the moment. "So I guess it's business as usual until further notice?"

"Yes." If business as usual means my life is turning into the plot of a *Riverdale* episode.

I lay Fia down on my bed, over the changing pad, and she smiles up at me with her cute little lips. My heart tingles with joy, and I realize that despite the chaos, this is the happiest I've ever been.

I don't have everything I want, but maybe I have everything I need.

CHAPTER TWENTY-ONE

I spend the rest of the morning cleaning up the apartment. I take Fia to the gym in her carrier and almost complete an entire hour of weights. Our first game is on Sunday against our biggest rival, the California Turkeys. (Really the Thunderbirds, but we hate them, so yeah. Turkeys.)

Now I'm driving home to shower, change, and eat before tonight's practice. I try not to think about Marli and the fact I haven't heard any news about her death. It doesn't mean the police aren't investigating, but I'd feel better if I knew where things stood. Have they ID'd her? Linked her to Tony?

There's nothing to do but wait now, and that includes waiting for Lara, who, in the midst of all this insanity, makes me feel happy. I just hope she's ready soon to take things to the next level. Not sure how much more buildup I can take.

By Sunday morning, I'm about to explode. Lara's stayed over the last few nights, and her warm soft body next to mine is torture. I can't count the number of times I've wanted to kiss her, touch her, make love to her. I haven't jerked off this much since I was sixteen. But all this is worth it because I know she's working through stuff, and she's doing it for us—me and Fia.

As for all the other things in my life, there haven't been any real developments other than Larry the lawyer released a press statement, making it clear that any news outlets reporting false information about me will be held liable and that we plan to make a big announcement in a few days. I'm guessing he means the paternity test.

I have to call and let him know I didn't go in for the blood work appointment. I just won't be able to tell him why. Linking this baby to Marli, and possibly Tony (I hope not), puts Fia at risk. Puts me and Lara at risk, too.

Then there's Flip. He's left two messages over the last few days, asking what the hell is going on. He's obviously seen all the news about Fia. I haven't called him back because I don't know what to tell him. He knows me. And like Lara, he knows when I'm lying. The last thing Flip needs right now is to be worrying about me and adding to his stress.

Still, I have to come up with something because I plan to drive out to see him tomorrow, right after class. It's my only window because I'm going to have one hell of a busy week between college, football, time at the Ranch, and Fia. Thankfully, one of our coworkers at the Ranch recommended a woman who runs an affordable daycare in her home.

Lara checked all the references and stopped by to meet the lady. Thumbs up.

I don't know what I would do without Lara. I feel like she's the piece of my life that's always been missing, and her fearlessness inspires me. She's watched Fia the last three nights, and I already see them bonding, which seems to be healing old wounds. Meanwhile, people's kindness is healing mine. Coach and his wife stopped by to check on us and offer support. Even Hector says he'll let Lara bring Fia into work during the day if necessary.

Everyone who matters is behind me, which makes it easier to accept that others aren't. For example, I ran into Nina yesterday as I was heading out. She took one look at me and Fia and rolled her eyes. I can't believe I didn't see through her earlier. She was never my friend. Just another person who wanted to use me.

As for Mike, he hasn't been around—new girl-friend of the week—and he keeps to himself at practice. Igor is his usual self, kind of in his own world, unaffected by any drama.

On the more positive side, the public is still making donations for Fia, which means not every-one is stupid enough to believe what they hear. And I'm smart enough to be grateful for them. I plan to open a college savings account for Fia with the money so at least I know her future is taken care of no matter what happens to me.

Look at me daddying like a pro.

In the space of one week, I went from being a single man with the weight of the world on his shoulders, to being a dad who feels like he has a world full of people lifting him up. One little person and one special woman, in particular, get the bulk of the credit.

I plan to carry that positivity into tonight's game. I'm in the starting lineup, and this time, I'm not going to drop the ball. Literally, of course.

"I'm going to kick ass tonight. Isn't that right, princess?" I look over at Fia, who's in her carrier on the floor, fascinated by a new purple pacifier I just bought her. Had to make a run to the grocery store to get a few supplies. Lara went back to her place to do some light cleaning since Fia and I are heading over for a late Sunday breakfast. Pancakes. I need to carb up for the game. Then Lara's taking Fia the rest of the day and bringing her to watch me play.

My phone rings, and I answer, thinking it might be Lara checking in, but I don't recognize the number. "Hello?"

"Who the fuck is this?" says a deep scratchy voice.

"You called me," I say.

"No shit. Because this is the last number my wife called."

Tony Rigatoni. This has to be him. My stomach tightens, and my heart rate spikes. I have to keep my cool. "Don't know what you're talking about. She probably dialed me by accident."

"You talked to her for ten seconds. I got the phone right here."

So Tony has her cell, the cell with the five thousand messages I left her. I can only hope Marli deleted them. Otherwise, we're fucked.

"I don't know, man," I say. "I get spam calls all the time. They go into my voicemail. Sorry I can't help you." I'm about to hang up because that's what any person would do if a stranger called asking about his wife.

"I'm gonna find you," he growls, "and when I do, I'm gonna get the truth outta ya."

"Look, I don't know you. I don't know your wife, so—"

"I gotta pair of pliers that say otherwise."

Wow. Straight to the chase. At least he didn't threaten me with a cheese grater. Then I'd know he means business.

"Pliers won't change my answer. Good luck with your wife."

"She's dead. And you're next."

The call ends, and then, yes, I feel my shit start to unwind. I'm about to lose it. *Stay calm, Dean.* I need a clear head because clearly, I need a new plan. I have no doubt this psycho is going to track me down using my phone number. And if the rumors are true about Tony, he's the sort of man who has the connections to do it quickly.

It's time to fight. And I'm suddenly not regretting growing up where I did. That hellhole taught me to push back, to defend myself and my brother, to not back down when someone wants to take everything from you. Maybe that's why I love football—it makes sense to me. It's an orchestrated battle, symbolic of what I've lived through to get to where I am.

But this Tony isn't playing a game, and neither am I.

I dig out Larry's card from my wallet.

"I'll go along with this, Dean, but I'm not a fan of your plan," Larry says, seated behind his big fancy desk. Today, instead of a suit, he's wearing my team's red and black jersey and a matching baseball cap. Glad he's a fan. Also glad he was willing to meet on such short notice. I called earlier, expecting to talk through this on the phone, but he happened to be in his office and told me to come over.

Despite the fact it's a Sunday, and the place is void of people, his law office isn't the grim, stale atmosphere I expected. There's a play area for kids near reception, and the common areas are filled with colorful art, bright lighting, and plants. I'm guessing by the numbers of desks and private offices, he must have an army working for him. Either way, the prestigious appearance immediately boosts my confidence. Larry must know what he's doing to have a practice like this.

And I bet he's expensive. I owe Hector and Coach for hiring him.

"I don't see a better plan," I say, rocking Fia in my arms while standing. She's been a gas bag the last thirty minutes, almost like her bowels know something bad is going down. "If I go to the police first, they'll want to play this out their way—maybe block me from going public or arrest me for withholding information. This is the *only* way to get the entire truth out. On my terms."

"It's a gamble," Larry says.

I've told him everything—attorney-client privilege—so I agree with his concerns. The risk is real. But I refuse to allow that piece of garbage to get away with killing Fia's mother. And I'm not about to live looking over my shoulder the rest of my life. It's time to take a stand.

"Tony Rigatoni is planning to come after me," I say. "My way will make him hit pause because if anything happens, the world will know it was him." My plan will force Tony to wait, and that will buy the authorities time to hunt him down. "I just need to run this by Lara and make sure she's okay with it. Then I need you on standby since I'm fairly sure the police will want to talk to me and Lara."

"I'll call the detective the moment this goes public. Better if we're proactive and offer your cooperation."

I like that Larry is looking out for me. "Thanks."

"You got it. But I want you to stick to the script, Dean."

"What script?"

"I'm going to tell you exactly what to say so you don't incriminate yourself."

I like that plan. And I like that I'm fighting back—against Tony, against the press, and against anyone who thinks I'm not a good father. "Lay it on me, Larry. But make it quick. Fia's naptime is overdue."

He smiles, flashing a very perfect set of white teeth. Probably veneers. "Let's do this."

CHAPTER TWENTY-TWO

"You're serious? You really want to do this?" Lara asks, sitting on her khaki love seat. This is the first time I've been to her place. It's a spacious in-law unit with two bedrooms, located on a ten-acre farm, just minutes from the Ranch. The floors are all hardwood, there's a fireplace, and the furniture looks like it came from one of those homey interior design magazines. Lara is clearly into floral patterns and red throw pillows—they're on the couch, love seat, and armchair. She even has red cushions on the chairs at her round dining room table in the corner. Looks nice. She's definitely been slumming it at my place, where we have very prestigious garage-sale décor.

Standing near the window, I fold my arms and look outside at the towering pine trees in her yard. "I am serious. And yes, I want to do this," I lie. I definitely don't want to. This is more of a need situation. "When Tony finds me, and I have no doubt he will, he'll take out anyone I'm with to punish me. That's what Marli said." Also, I don't want to go into hiding or run or let him get away with murder. Again. "I'd say I'm being paranoid except for the fact I've witnessed his handiwork."

"Agreed." Lara exhales with a worried look. "I'm in. But we have to be smart. Let's change our routine for a few weeks. I can book us an Airbnb in the area. We can maybe rent a different car or something. The name of the game is making it difficult for Tony to find you."

"I love that plan. I just hope this is the right choice. If anything happened to you or Fia—"

"Don't you worry, Dean. We're a team. We got this." She smiles, and her gaze drops down to my groin. "But since you got me into this mess, you are going to have to make it up to me."

"Are you asking for sexual favors as compensation for dragging you into my horribly messed-up life?"

"Maybe." Her smile grows into a full-blown display of happiness, and I can't stop myself from mirroring her. I think this means she's ready to take things to the next level.

Yes!

And…nooo! My excitement is immediately hampered by the fact that I need to get to the stadium. "Can I pay you after the game? I gotta get going." There's my press conference, warm-up, and then the game.

"No," Lara says.

"No?"

"One installment won't be sufficient. You'll need to pay me several times."

I press my hand over my heart. "You really think so little of my skills?"

She raises a light brown brow.

"I promise you'll be offering a credit halfway through."

She laughs, and her cheeks turn red. "Okay, big boy. Off you go to the game." She hops up and throws her arms around me. I think she's going to kiss me, but instead she clings tightly. "Be careful, Dean. That crazy asshole might be at the game."

That's a cliché. Mimi would never let that happen.

I pull away and look down at her beautiful face. "He'd be stupid to try anything in front of so many people." The press will be there in spades. The stadium is sold out. "Tell Fia I love her when she wakes up from her nap."

Lara blinks up at me. "You love her?"

"I do." Even if I'm shocked to hear the words come out of my mouth, I know what I feel. That little girl stole my heart the first moment I held her stinky little body.

"How about me?" she asks, her voice saturated with vulnerability.

"You're kinda ugly, so I'll need to get back to you on that."

Her jaw drops.

"I'm joking!"

Lara smacks my arms. "That wasn't funny, Dean!"

"Sorry."

She stares up at me expectantly with her wide brown eyes. I know what she wants to hear, but I'm not ready to say it.

Instead, I grab her shoulders, pull her into me, and kiss her hard. Her lips are stiff for a few seconds, but then she opens to me, and our tongues lash together. My body is screaming to take her, kiss her, run my tongue up and down the inside of her thigh. I want the taste of her in my mouth when I'm playing tonight.

"Wah! Wah!" screams Fia from the porta-crib I brought over, now assembled in Lara's spare bedroom.

And there's the cockblocker right on cue. I break our kiss. "Payment in full after the game. I promise."

Lara licks her lips. "Okay, but don't be late with it. I charge interest." She flicks a thumb over her shoulder. "I should answer the call before she implodes."

"See you at the game."

"I'll be in the front row with bells on. And a screaming baby."

I love it. I love how together, Lara, Fia, and I have become a team. Life feels different now. Not to say that on our own, we were nothing. That's not true. But we've become a sort of family, as untraditional as it is, and it's made us all stronger. I can't afford to mess this up or lose them.

When I get to the stadium, I'm not surprised to see the press clogging the parking lot with their vans. They've almost become a fixture in my life. What *does* shock me is that my team, minus a few, are gathered outside by the entrance of the locker room.

Are they holding a joint press conference? I haven't been informed of anything.

I park in one of the last spots at the very end, grab my gear, and head toward the swarm. I'm immediately bombarded with questions from the press, but I've learned to pretend they're not even there.

"Coach? What's going on?" I ask, coming up to him. He's at the center of it all, looking stoic.

"We heard you're making a statement and wanted to be here to support you. As any good team would."

I'm blown away. "But you guys don't need to get mixed up in this."

"No, but we want to," he says. "Thus, the reason we're all out here showing support."

I don't know what to say. My gaze glides over the faces of my teammates. "Thank you. Really, thank you. But I'd feel a lot better if you were not a part of this."

They have no idea I'm about to call out Tony. This is not a political stand. This is not a frivolous PR stunt. I'm fighting for my life as well as my daughter's and Lara's.

"Get on with it, Norland!" one of the guys yells out. "We gotta game to win." The chorus of teammates join in, and I look at Coach, pleading with my eyes for them not to do this.

"You heard 'em," he says. "Get on with it."

I inhale slowly. "All right…" I turn and stand with two firm feet to face the press. "Ladies. Gentlemen. Teammates. I'm here to make a statement and…" I don't want to mess this up, so I pull out the piece of paper with the speech Larry provided. "I am speaking today because I want the world to know the truth about me, my baby, and her mother. A crime has been committed, and the responsible party must be held accountable." I go on to tell everyone about meeting Marli and how she said she was mourning the loss of her marriage. Me? I was mourning the loss of a dream. I go on to explain how Marli showed up last Sunday with a surprise.

Everyone is silent and listening up until the part when I disclose the real reason Marli left Fia with me: she was married to Tony "the rolling pin" Rigatoni and on the run.

Mutters and mumbles break out among the crowd, including my teammates standing behind me.

"A few days ago," I say, "Marli returned and

asked to meet, which is how I learned the truth about her dangerous situation. All she asked of me was to protect Fia's identity so that her husband wouldn't learn about Marli's infidelity. Basically, a death sentence for all of us. Marli believed that Fia is mine but wasn't absolutely sure, nor did she care. She begged me to ensure that Tony would never be a part of Fia's life no matter what. Minutes after I left Marli alone in her motel room, Tony killed her with a ladle."

Tears well in my eyes. *Dammit, Norland. You can't cry. You'll never hear the end of it.* But I can't stop myself from feeling what I do. None of this should have happened.

I straighten my back, determined to take it like a man. If they want to laugh, so be it. "Tony found my phone number on Marli's cell and reached out to me today. He made it clear he intends to kill me. He does not know about Fia, but it was only a matter of time.

"That's why I decided to go public today. I want everyone to know what happened to Fia's mom. She did not deserve to die like that. I want everyone to know who is responsible, and in case I'm murdered with, say, a spork or other random kitchen utensil, you'll know who's behind it. I hope the authorities will place the full force of their efforts into catching this vicious man, even if he's connected to powerful people, before anyone else becomes a victim of his ladle. Or rolling pin. Or whatever weird crap he's into that week."

I stand still for several long moments, noticing the absolute silence in the air. I look over my shoulder at my teammates only to find an ocean of shocked, horrified, and blank faces.

"Okay!" Coach claps his hands. "Good talk. Everyone inside. Chop-chop!"

The team eagerly complies, kind of reminding me of forest creatures fleeing a wildfire.

I follow them inside and catch up with Coach. He looks like he wants to piss himself—stiff back, pale face, sweaty brow. "Next time a murderer is after you, how about a heads-up, son?"

"Fair point." Though, I tried to warn him. Maybe I should have tried harder. "You want me to go? I'll understand if you do."

"Hell no, son. I'll never hear the end of it from Jo if I don't give you your shot tonight, and, frankly, I'm not changing my lineup because of that worthless SOB. I mean really? Who kills a woman with a ladle? Sicko."

Truth. "You're serious? I can play?"

"Just don't screw up the game tonight, Norland. We've all placed our chips on you."

And there's the pressure, pedestal, and confidence-undermining shebang. Awesome. It's going to take a miracle to get me through tonight.

"Go suit up," he adds.

"Yep. Got it. Game on, Coach." I head straight to the bathroom and throw up. I can already feel the weight of the pedestal crushing me. *I'm fucked. So very fucked.*

CHAPTER TWENTY-THREE

Sixty seconds until the kickoff, and I've tried every trick in the book to get my head straight. I did visualizations of calming streams, I thought about how the people in my life are depending on me, and I reminded myself how much I want this. I've pushed on every possible angle, but the weight is still there, suffocating me.

Come on, Norland. Get it together. But the loud cheers of the fans fill my ears to a point where I can hardly hear myself think. I don't dare look at anything other than the green grass below my feet. God forbid I see a fan smiling in my direction, hoping great things for me tonight.

I get into position, one fist planted in the soft moist turf. *You can do this, Norland. Focus. Focus.* The sweat accumulates on the small of my back. My stomach knots into a painful ball.

I hear the slap of a foot against the ball, and play starts. I run and try to think of my training, of the plays, of my team.

Suddenly, I'm running and have no idea where

the ball is. One of my teammates calls my name, and when I turn my head, I'm greeted with a three-hundred-pound tank rolling over me.

I fly back, and the ref blows the whistle. I don't know why that guy sacked me, but I'm guessing it was an accident. I got in his way because I'm not paying attention.

"*Choo* okay?" Igor holds out a hand and pulls me up.

"Yeah." I shake my head. "I just got a little turned around."

He slaps my helmet. "*Geet chor* head out of your ass, Norland."

We get into formation. My team is still in possession of the ball, which means I have to be ready. If the ball is passed to me, I have to catch it. There're no more chances after this.

Our quarterback makes the call, and I run through the Turkeys' defenses. I can't believe it was so easy. The rush of a wide-open field takes over. I pump my legs and fly like the wind. I glance over my shoulder and spot the quarterback exactly where he should be. We make eye contact, and his arm winds back and then snaps.

I see the ball coming straight toward me.

And then…fuck. I'm out of the zone. Just like that, I'm hyperaware of the crowd yelling my name, cheering me on. The pain seeps into my chest, and I can't breathe.

Wake up, Norland. Catch the damned ball. Catch

it. I slow my pace and adjust my trajectory to make the catch and then—

Ooph! My body flies left, and I land with a thump on the grass. The pain shoots through my shoulder, ribs, and hip. I'm seeing stars, and in the back of my mind I hear the ref call the incomplete pass.

A large guy from the other team looms over me and holds out his hand to help me up. "You still breathing, dirtbag?"

"Yeah," I groan, noting how I absolutely hate being run over by men who outweigh me by a hundred pounds. That fucking hurt.

He helps me up, and I thank him accordingly. "Dick."

He chuckles and walks away. Meanwhile, my teammates are making nervous side glances. I think they know I was about to screw up that pass either way.

The coach blows his whistle for a timeout, which is highly unusual this early in the game. He calls me over.

Shit. He's taking me out already? No. No. No. This is my dream. I've worked hard for this. I know I'm capable of spinning this plate.

I pop off my helmet and jog over, knowing the entire world is watching. An exaggeration. It's probably only a million people if you count the cable subscribers.

"Hey, Coach."

"Norland, I gotta pull you out."

If I were him, I'd be making the same call. But I'm not him. I'm me. And this is my dream. I've got to fight. "Just give me one more shot, please. I can do this. I can get my head in the game."

"Son, this isn't about you. The team—"

"That's why I'm begging to stay in. For them. They've stepped up for me, and I can't go out failing them." I mean it, too. "This is my dream, but that dream is helping my team go as far as it can."

I look over Coach's shoulder and spot Lara standing there with Fia in her arms. Lara looks worried. Fia looks like she always has—adorable. My heart melts. *My two girls*, I think proudly, feeling overcome with emotion. I love them. And they love me. I think? I'm not sure if babies can actually love.

"Coach, one more play, and if I screw up, I'll take myself out of the game. No questions asked."

Coach shakes his head. "Fine. Go."

"One second." I run past him toward the first row of bleachers.

"Dean, what are you doing?" Lara asks. The entire stadium is staring.

"I need Fia. Just for a second." I set down my helmet and hold out my arms.

"But you're in the middle of the game and—"

"Baby, please," I command, flicking my hands so Lara will hand her over.

"Uh, okay…" Lara carefully lowers Fia in her

pink onesie over the railing.

I take Fia's warm tiny frame into my arms and instantly feel it: that wave of peacefulness and calm. This is what I needed. She's the cure to my anxiety. She's my reason for not giving up.

I kiss her sweet little cheek. "I love you, baby girl. Daddy's going to make you proud and keep you safe. Always." I hand her back to Lara, who's all teary-eyed.

I grab my helmet and look over my shoulder. The entire stadium is silent.

"Sorry, I just needed to hold my daughter." *Why is everyone sniffling?* Even Coach is wiping under his eyes.

I walk to my spot on the field, the crowd staring as if I were an alien.

"What?" I mutter under my breath, getting into position for the next play. "Haven't you ever seen a dad kiss his baby?"

Igor slaps me on the back. "Man, that was really cute."

I frown. "Can we play? The clock is ticking."

Both teams get into formation. My chest has never felt lighter. My life has never been better. Tonight, this moment, is perfect. Well, except for the psycho killer after me, but besides that…perfect. I don't even care if we win the game. I'm just in love with being here. Playing the game I love with a team I love. My daughter in the stadium, being held by the woman I love.

Life doesn't get any better, and I'm going to savor all five hundred miles around the track.

⤞ ⤝

"Good game, Norland!" My teammates take the time to clap me on the back as we enter the locker room. Not only did we win tonight, but I brought in three touchdowns. Our rival team, the Turkeys, is going home in total defeat.

I pull off my helmet and shove it into my locker.

"Norland," Coach comes up behind me, "now that was some game. Good job."

"Thanks." I smile proudly. It feels incredible to help the team start out the season with a win. It'll set the pace for us. "I appreciate you giving me my shot."

"Glad I did. I'm even going to forgive that stunt you pulled."

"Stunt?" I ask.

"The baby kissing. You planning to run for office or something?"

I laugh. "Sorry. I just needed a second to reset."

"Well, it worked. But next time, get your smoochies in before the game starts."

"Yes, Coach."

He walks away, and I strip off my uniform. I wrap my towel around my waist and am about to hit the showers when my cell rings. I'm eager to get washed up and go find Lara and Fia, but I check it anyway. It's Hector.

"Hey, Hector. What's up?"

"Saw the game! Just calling to congratulate you, Dean. You really looked like you were in the zone tonight. That was some win."

"I focused on enjoying the ride. Just like you said."

"I'm proud of you. Also, the Ranch's sale is complete, and I'm leaving early tomorrow, so this is also goodbye. By the way, I made sure you've got a position here after you graduate—if you want it."

"That's, uh, really nice of you, Hector."

"Just be sure to give the new owner a chance. Jed's young, but he's smart and ambitious like you. He's also a little rough around the edges, but what can you expect from a Texas cowboy?"

I met Jed for a brief second this week when I stopped by to collect my paycheck. He seemed okay. "Thanks, Hector. For everything. I hope you find what you're looking for on that yacht."

He laughs. "Bye, Dean. And congratulations again."

We end the call, and I know in the back of my mind why Hector said what he did about the job. His goal in life has never been about obtaining wealth or power. It's about love, like he said. I think he saw me playing tonight, and he knows I have some tough choices ahead.

If I play the rest of the season like I played tonight, I'll be drafted. But where does that leave Fia? I can't take a baby on the road. And what about Lara? I can't expect her to become a full-time single mom while I'm away for weeks. Then there's Flip. Who'll look after him? And what about college? I can't play football forever, and finishing my education is the rational choice.

Yet I can't stop thinking about how much I want this. My passion is football, and if I'm lucky enough to play in the NFL, I can't pass it up.

There has to be a solution.

And I think I just figured it out. It's the perfect solution for everyone.

Filled with happiness, I puff out my chest. *Damn, I'm good.* I walk through the middle of the locker room toward the showers and yank off my towel.

Time to fuck with my teammates.

"See it and weep, guys." I smile, letting my big dick swing in the air.

"Fuck you, Norland," one of my teammates calls out, followed by me being pegged in the back with wads of towels and sweaty jerseys.

"Just showing off my dad bod." I chuckle and hit the showers. *I'm back, bitches.*

CHAPTER TWENTY-FOUR

I'm walking out of the locker room, anxious to find Lara and Fia, who should be somewhere near her car on the other side of the press mob, when a familiar face blocks my path.

"Hey, Dean," says Dannie, smiling like the she-demon she is. She's wearing a low-cut black T-shirt and skintight jeans.

And I couldn't care less.

"What do you want, Dannie?" I say in my coldest possible voice.

"I was in the neighborhood. Okay, I came with friends to watch the game. Amazing job. Anyway, since I'm here, I wanted to apologize for that huge misunderstanding. I honestly thought I was helping Fia and doing the right thing."

"You know," I say, "I've given a lot of thought to what would make a person accuse a dad of stealing his own daughter."

"Well," she chuckles judgmentally, "you still don't actually know if she's yours."

"She's not stolen, Dannie."

"True. Good point. And that's why I'm here. After tonight, I think your stock went up, and I'm willing to offer two hundred thousand for a spokesperson deal." She steps in close, our bodies almost touching. "I'll throw in a few other perks, too," she whispers, attempting to sound seductive.

"You didn't let me finish," I say, keeping up the disdainful tone. "I finally figured out why you went on social media and tried to turn the world against me." I narrow my eyes. "You figured you could use my name to get free publicity. And what better way to show how dedicated your daycare is to the well-being of children than to make the world believe you helped save a stolen baby."

Dannie shrugs. "Well, you were no good to me as a single-daddy spokesperson if you weren't going to keep Fia. But hey, look how great it all worked out. You're the belle of the ball. Hot Daddy Dean again."

"They took her away from me," I snarl.

"You got her back."

"You are an evil human being. I wouldn't even let you watch my houseplant." I walk away.

"Fuck you, Dean," she says.

I mutter under my breath, "No. Fuck you, Dannie." She didn't even notice the news camera right behind her, waiting to interview me. They heard everything. Probably recorded it, too.

I smile. Dannie is definitely about to get some publicity. Karma is a bitch.

I leave behind a mob of reporters who are talking to the Coach and my teammates. My eyes scan the parking lot until they lock on the two most beautiful faces on the planet. *My girls.*

Lara rushes over and greets me with a big hug, sandwiching Fia between us. "Dean, that was awesome!"

"Careful. Don't squish my lucky charm," I say and give Lara a kiss. I then peck Fia on the top of her soft little head.

"Why don't we go out to celebrate?"

"Sorry. I'm meeting up with the guys. You can sit for me tonight, right?" I watch Lara's happy expression melt into disappointment.

I need to work on my jokes. "I'm kidding. I already have plans. With you. In your bed. And a certain payment you owe me." I wink.

She smiles. "You're mean, Dean Norland."

"Or am I a sexy, sexy man who just made three touchdowns?"

"That, too."

"Can we stop by my place, though? I want to pick up some fresh clothes for Fia and myself." Tomorrow, we'll figure out where we're going to stay and the next steps after that. Larry already left a message, saying he got in touch with that detective. I have to meet him at the station tomorrow to make a statement. It's going to get messy, but I was expecting that.

"Dean, I'm really nervous. What if that Tony

guy shows up at your apartment?"

"He'd have to be a complete moron to try anything. For all he knows, my apartment is being watched, and so are we." That was the point of going public. The police will be looking for Tony, and if he's smart, he's going to keep a low profile. "Mike and Igor also invited a bunch of people over so there'll be too many witnesses." As for Lara's place, Tony might've seen her face during the game, but he doesn't know who she is. Yet. We should be safe for tonight, but all the same, I'm going to keep an eye out for him.

I lean down and press my lips to Lara's soft mouth, lingering a bit. My need to take her to bed is instant. "We need to hurry. I'm pumped full of testosterone and victory. If I don't fuck you soon, I'm going to explode."

"Dean Norland, that is so unromantic." She pauses. "And so very hot. I'm in."

LARA

I'm in good spirits when I pull up to Dean's place with Fia in the back seat of my SUV, but I'm also on my guard despite the fact that Dean's just ahead of me in his truck and there are still several news crews parked out front. I think one of the crews even followed us from the stadium.

Dean doesn't seem to notice them lurking, hovering, yelling out stupid questions, but I do. They're annoying as hell. Except for right now. I feel safer with them around. I saw what that psycho-creep Tony did to Fia's mother, and while I fully back Dean's choice to go public, I know it comes with risk. Until Tony is caught, we have to be careful.

Aside from that, I'm currently experiencing a full-blown, raging case of love. That moment in the stadium when Dean completely stopped the game just to kiss his little girl and tell her he loves her, melted me to the core. I can't help thinking if every dad was like him, the world would be a much different place.

And if anyone thought for a second that the baby-smoochie moment made Dean look like a pussy, those thoughts were immediately erased when he kicked ass and took names on the field.

I honestly hate football, but even I was losing my mind watching Dean play. It was insane! He dodged tackles, he ducked tackles, and he even jumped over some guy who was going for his knees. Jerk. That would have really hurt Dean if he weren't so quick on his feet. The other team couldn't touch him.

By the end of the game, I swear I was ready to drop my panties right there and try to tackle him myself. So hot. And that muscled ass? Jesus, it should be illegal for a man's ass to look like that. How am I ever going to concentrate again? *Lara, have you finished that report?*

No, sorry. I'm doodling an image of Dean's ass.

Lara, shouldn't you be watching the road while you're driving?

Yes. I should. But I'm too busy thinking of Dean's ass.

Those are the kinds of conversations I can look forward to in the near future.

I park around the back of the complex next to Dean's truck, which he'll leave here for a few days.

Dean walks over to help with Fia, whom he grabs from the back. "Let's make this fast and get out of here. Lots to do." He winks.

I don't know if he's eager to get back to my place for sex or if he's nervous about Tony showing up. Either way, I agree.

Dean looks at Fia. "And no beer for you, little girl. No flirting either. Those boys are much too old for you." He chuckles and looks at me. "Just practicing for when she's older."

I can't imagine what Dean will be like when Fia's old enough to date. I bet he'll scare off all the boys. Honestly, I won't blame him. There is something special about her. Maybe it's her big wonderous eyes. Maybe it's her cherublike face or the way she smiles all the time, like she's watching us and enjoying herself. I don't know, but this week, as difficult and tragic as it's been, has helped me in ways I never imagined.

I have love to thank for that, I think. When it clicked for me with Dean, it clicked hard. I just knew this was meant to be. Him. Me. Fia. I'll never get my daughter back, but I have found my home with these two.

Dean cradles Fia in his large arms. He's such a huge guy with big biceps, it always makes Fia look like a miniature doll.

I so want him. He's got to be the hottest dad in the world. "Let's hurry. I'm itching for some payment."

Dean flashes a grin. "Stop. You'll give me a boner."

I shake my head. He's hilarious. Most of the time.

I follow him up the stairs. The two of us are chatting away, talking about options for dinner at my place and how to get Fia to bed early tonight. I've never been so grateful to have two bedrooms.

Dean reaches for the front door of his apartment, totally oblivious to the reporters running toward us down the hall. I'm eager to duck inside and avoid them until something strikes me as weird. There's no noise inside.

"Wait. Didn't you say there's a party—"

I'm too late. Because Dean steps inside. "Lara, don't come in here," he says.

"Shut up," says a deep voice.

I don't know what I'm thinking, other than I'm not about to leave Fia and Dean, because I step inside. *A much, much wiser choice than running for help, Lara. You idiot!*

Running was probably our only hope.

CHAPTER TWENTY-FIVE

"You. Get over there and join your friends." Tony Rigatoni waves a very large gun at my face. He's not a big man, but there's something about his eyes that screams *crazy person!* It's hard to describe other than they lack any sign of human warmth. Apart from that, he looks like your average Joe—short brown hair, medium build, and a paunch. Nothing menacing or scary about him, including his outfit. Brown pants, a gray golf shirt, and a Members Only jacket.

Okay, there is the gun, so I guess that makes him scary. My eyes gravitate toward a figure lying on the couch.

Now that makes him horrifying. Apparently, Tony has killed one of Dean's teammates. Or could be a roommate. I really can't tell from the angle of the hand mixer sticking out of the guy's face.

What is with this guy and kitchen stuff? Maybe his mother was a mean chef.

Everyone else is gagged and has their feet and hands bound with rope. I count two girls and three guys, including the dead guy. I glance at the body again and realize it's Mike, Dean's roommate.

Oh no...

"Tony," says Dean, holding Fia tightly, "your fight's with me. Not anyone else."

Tony's brown eyes twitch, and he jerks the gun at Dean and me. "I'll give you both five seconds to put down that baby, dump your phones, and sit on the floor."

"We can't put a baby on that carpet. It's dirty," I say.

Tony cocks his gun.

"Okay. Carpet it is." I go to help Dean, who doesn't want to let go of the baby. He gives me a look like he wants me to stop.

"Get behind me," he whispers, and then he looks at Tony. "Why don't you tell me what you want, because you'll be living on the run the rest of your life if you kill us. And for what? Did you even love Marli?"

I want to point out that Tony is up the creek either way because he's already killed Mike. Marli, too. Tony's screwed the pooch on this one.

"What's love got to do with it?" Tony says. "Marli was my property."

Dean shrugs. "I had an old car once that just became a money pit. I would have been much better off trading it in for something more reliable, but did I? No. I just kept throwing money at it, and—"

"Shut the fuck up!" Tony yells. "Get on your

knees."

"What are you going to do with the baby?" I ask.

"Not your problem," Tony says.

"You can't take care of her—it's a full-time job. You'll be on the run. I can just leave her outside, okay? It'll take two seconds. Someone will find her and take her to a good home." I don't know if that's true, but at least she'll have a chance.

"She's not even mine. Why do I care if she lives?" Tony growls.

It dawns on me that he intends to kill us all. Or as many as he can manage with the supplies in Dean's kitchen.

"She might be yours," I say. "Don't you want to know for sure before you…" My voice fades. I can't say the words.

"All I know is she came out of that whore of my wife. The kid'll just grow up to be trash like her mom."

Ouch. Harsh.

I can tell that Tony's reached his limit, and our attempt to buy more time has ended. I hoped someone would show up for the party or one of those pesky reporters might knock on the door and distract Tony long enough for me to make a move. God knows Dean has his hands full with precious cargo.

Dean and I exchange glances. I'm not sure, but I think we've both reached the same conclusion.

Only a miracle is going to save us.

I walk over to join the group crammed together on the other side of the living room in front of the sliding glass door. Dean crouches and sets Fia on the carpeted floor. She instantly begins screaming bloody murder.

"Make her stop!" Tony says.

"I can't do that without picking her up," Dean says.

I'm about to say I'll get her because I want Dean to have a chance to use that famous speed and powerful body to steamroll this guy, but Dean is too quick, eager to protect his baby daughter. He scoops her up and starts to soothe her with a back rub.

Suddenly, there's a knock at the door.

"You go sit down. No one makes a sound, or I'll shoot you." Tony waves his gun right at Dean.

Are we saved by the bell? *Please be the police looking to interview us. Please, please, please.*

Tony waits until we're seated and in position at the furthest edge of the room, making it impossible to rush at him without getting shot first.

The person at the door knocks again, and Tony goes to answer it.

"Yeah. What do you want?" Tony says.

I hear a sound, like something smashing into flesh and bone. There's a grunt, followed by a groan. I know in my heart that whoever was at the door is victim number two for the night.

I have to do something. I have to get that gun

away from Tony. I know he'll shoot me, but what choice do I have? Once, a very long time ago, I didn't stand up and fight for someone I loved very much. She was my flesh and blood, and I just gave her away when I should've made a stand. But I didn't. And I've lived with nothing but regret. I refuse to go back to that place in my heart ever again.

I hop to my feet and rush toward the small entryway, ready to jump Tony the second he comes into view. I collide with a tall body and fly back, landing on my ass.

I look up and see a guy who looks like a thinner version of Dean—tall, hazel eyes, and broad shoulders.

Dean rushes over with a crying Fia. "Flip?"

DEAN

My little brother is standing in my apartment, and Tony Rigatoni is out cold on the floor.

I reach for Flip and hug him tight, trying not to crush a hysterical Fia. "I don't know what you're doing here, but, man, am I happy to see you." I release him and bask in the wonderful absurd luck that he showed up when he did. "What are you doing here?"

"I left rehab."

Crap. He did this last time—said all the right

things, pretended to follow the program, took his meds. He behaved just long enough so he could get out early. Which means he's back on drugs again.

My heart sinks. But now is not the time to get into it. Mike is dead, people are tied up in my living room, and there's an unconscious killer on my floor.

"No, Dean," Flip says, reading my thoughts. "It's not like that."

"I wasn't—"

"I see it on your face, bro. You think I'm free and looking to party. But I'm not. I'm working hard. I got clean and earned a spot at a halfway house."

"You have?"

"You'd know that if you bothered answering my calls."

"I tried calling you back, but—" I run a hand through my hair. "You're right. I should've tried harder. I'm sorry."

"Don't be. I'm glad you've been MIA lately. It made me realize I needed to do this on my own. I needed to prove I could make it through the program and stay clean on the outside."

This is amazing. In the past, he only did the bare minimum so he could get out and go back to drugs. "I'm really proud of you."

"Guys," Lara barks, picking up Tony's gun off the floor and shoving into her waistband, making her look dangerous. *So hot!* "Can you save the family reunion for later? I need help untying everyone. And it would be great if someone called the police before Mr. Kitchen Magic wakes up." She looks at Flip. "By the way, it's great to meet you." She goes right in and hugs Flip. "How did that even happen?" She glances at Tony on the floor.

Flip shrugs. "He opened the door, and I recognized him right away. The news showed his face right after you held that conference before the game."

Finally. Those stupid reporters are good for something. "What did you hit him with?" I ask.

"My fists. Finally paid off growing up in that shitty neighborhood." Flip bobs his head at Tony, looking proud of his handiwork. For the first time in a long time there's life in his eyes. He looks good. Healthy.

"Fia, meet your uncle Flip." I hand over my crying daughter.

"No. I can't hold her…" He takes her anyway, and Fia immediately stops crying.

"She likes you." We might have a future sitter. Not now, of course, but I can be hopeful. Today has been a day of miracles, after all. I'm alive. My family's okay. And Tony is no longer a threat. Plus, touchdowns.

I look at the unconscious piece of shit on my floor and give him a hard kick to the ribs. "That's for Marli."

CHAPTER TWENTY-SIX
LARA

Dressed in a white T-shirt and a pair of black boxer briefs, Dean slides between my champagne-colored satin sheets and sits against the headboard next to me, smelling sexy as ever. Baby lotion and mint toothpaste mixed with his natural woodsy scent. He looks exhausted, not that I can blame him. What a freaking day—press conferences, a football game, and nearly dying.

I'll just have to forgive him for not bothering to check out what I've got hidden underneath my floral comforter: pink panties and my pink satin PJ top.

"Wow. Fia must've been tired," I say. "It only took you two minutes to get her to sleep."

"We've all had a very long day," he says, shrugging off his awesome daddy skills. The man is a natural.

"I'm still blown away that your brother showed up like that." I didn't used to believe in divine intervention, but after today, I'm going to start.

"Neither can I. It was a close call." The cheery light in Dean's hazel eyes dulls.

"What is it?" I ask.

"Nothing. It's just, I've spent my entire life rescuing Flip and…"

I don't know much about Flip other than what's been made public as part of Dean's story. "And? How does it feel to have him rescue you for once?"

"Like I'm living in a dream—the type that's too good to be true."

"Oh, poor you. Is your life just too awesome to handle now? Must suck." I grin.

"No. I'm serious. I've lived my life being focused on having a plan to get me to a goal. It was all about buckling down, responsibilities, and making sacrifices."

"You're a hard worker. I respect that about you." I've never met anyone as driven as Dean.

"Yeah, but I think I got used to it. I definitely didn't believe I'd ever be happy, so I was just shooting for a life that wouldn't be a constant struggle."

I never really saw that in Dean, but now I get it—why he never flirted back or let people in. He was too focused on digging himself out of a hole he didn't want to be in. He wanted something better.

"And now?" I ask. "How do you feel?"

He turns his head, and the look in his eyes makes goosebumps explode all over my skin. "I feel…fucking wonderful, but I know it's not just because I played a good game of football. Which I did." He flashes a gloating grin.

Good for him. He's worked hard and should enjoy his success. "You really looked happy on the field tonight."

"Yeah, but here's the thing: If you asked me to choose between football or you guys, I'd pick you two. Because I know I can't be happy, really happy, unless you're both in my life."

"I'm not asking you to choose."

"I know."

"So then?" I'm confused.

"I want it all, but only if you do, too. Your all. My all. Us all."

I'm still confused. "All what?"

He takes my hand. "You have a dream of running your own winery; I have my dream of playing pro and finishing college. Somewhere in the middle of all that is us and a baby that wasn't part of the plan. But now that I have her, I'll do anything for her. Just like I'd do anything for you."

His words melt my insides. I'll never get used to hearing this big, jacked, fiercely masculine guy speak with so much strength and confidence while also being vulnerable. I have no idea how he pulls it off, but he does. It's incredibly sexy.

"I would do anything for you, too, Dean. I'd do anything for you both, which is totally insane given how fast everything's happened." We haven't even had sex yet. "But I know in my heart how special you guys are. So tell me what you want."

"I want us to make a plan."

"A plan?"

"Yeah. I want us to make a plan. Together. But the goal has to be living the happiest life we can. As a family."

I think I'm following what he's saying, but I can tell this is new territory for him. He's trying to open up.

I inhale slowly and choose my words carefully. This is important, and I don't want to mess it up. "I think what you're getting at is that I love you and you love me, and you don't want either of us to give up our dreams while we raise that beautiful little baby together. Am I right?"

He nods.

"Okay. Sounds good," I say.

"You sure?" He sounds shocked.

"Yeah. What's the big deal? We tackle it as a team." If I've learned anything this week, Dean and I make a great team. We've both helped each other move past some pretty ugly obstacles. And don't get me started about our chemistry. We've got more than I can take, and then some.

"But," he says, "I'll have classes, and you'll have work, then—"

"Dean, we got this. Let's just...make it happen."

His jaw drops. "That's my line."

I shrug. "Now it's our line."

He leans into me and presses his mouth to mine. I savor the feel of his warm lips and tongue dancing against mine. We've kissed before, but not like this. Not with so much connection and passion. The trust between us has opened up a whole new world.

I slide my hand to his short beard, enjoying the rough texture under my fingertips, and gaze into his eyes. I can't believe this is my guy. My person. I don't think I could have asked for a hotter mess of awesome man.

"I just need you to say it." I grin.

"Say what? That if you ever put your life at risk like that again, I'll come after you with a whisk?"

Ugh. Dean. The jokes. "Your timing needs work."

"Okay. Point taken." His expression turns serious. "What if I said that I love you, I am so thankful you gave me and Fia a chance to be a part of your life, and I'd really like to marry you. Doesn't have to be right away, but whenever you're ready. How's that?"

My eyes tear up, and I push back, diving head-first into happy sobs. "I think that's pretty good. But I really can't say yes to the cow until I've tried the milk."

"And you say my timing with jokes is bad?"

"Sorry." *Not sorry.* I had to say something to keep myself from ruining the moment. Crying is not sexy. At least when I do it. Imagine a turtle choking on a sour lemon.

"Let's see if this is funny." He grabs me and starts tickling my ribs.

"What! What are you doing?" I laugh hysterically, partially pissed off. I hate being tickled. "Stop it. Stop." I can't help laughing, though.

He flips me over and props me up on my hands and knees. "Mmm…nice panties."

"What in the world are you…oh!" Dean presses his hand between my thighs, and my eyes go wide. The sudden foreplay isn't unwelcome—not even a little—but I wasn't expecting it. And why does he have me facing away. "Dean, what are you doing?"

"It's better this way. Trust me." His hand goes right for that sweet, sensitive spot, and my body bucks.

It's been weeks since I've had any form of release, but it's been over a year since I've been with anyone. I can't deny his touch feels amazing, but… "I want to look at you. I want you to kiss me."

"No, you don't," he says bluntly.

Okay. Now he's being too strange, even for me. I twist my body and face him. "What's going on?" I say, getting a little annoyed.

He throws his head back. "Why can't you just trust me?"

"Because we've never had sex, and now you're acting weird. What are you hiding?"

"You really want to know?"

"Yes. I do. I'd like to know why you're ruining

this." I've dreamed of being with him for months.

"All right." He gets to his knees and lowers his underwear, exposing his huge, erect cock.

Oh crap. That's huge. I swallow down a dry lump in my throat. "Well, yeah. That's, um, pretty intense, Dean."

"I told you to trust me." He snaps up his waistband, not that his underwear does much to hide his monster cock.

I do not want, nor shall I ever, ask about his previous sexual experiences that have led him to believe that getting me hot and bothered first, without seeing his penis, is the answer. But I will say this, "I think you were right. Half payment is a good place to start." I'd like to be able to walk tomorrow.

EPILOGUE

"Oh fuck. Oh fuck, that's good. Don't stop." I'm breathing so hard, I think I might pass out.

"Not stopping. Not stopping." Dean's behind me, thrusting deep and gripping my hips like he's holding on for dear life.

I tilt my hips up and back, welcoming him to go deeper as the friction of his long, thick cock pushes me to my limit. "Yes. Right there." My mind is spinning out of control, and my body feels like it's about to combust. Every time he pulls out and slams back in, I see stars. I lose my breath. I want more.

We have sex every chance we get, which is only a handful of times a week, because we're both exhausted, but trust me, if I could get more of him, I would. Especially because it took over a month to, well, work up to it. Part of the issue had to do with nerves. The other part is because he really is huge.

Now, another two months later, we've found our groove; I can't get enough. Shower. Bed. Floor. Not the kitchen though. Never the kitchen. Too many triggers.

"Fuck. I need to go deeper." His voice is gruff and low. But I'm already raw and ready.

"I have to come. I can't wait." I pant my words, enjoying the sinful pressure and intense friction.

Dean bows his large body over my back and cups my heavy breasts with his large hands. He only does that when he's given himself permission to come because he knows I'm close. Very thoughtful.

"Now. Oh, God. Now," I say, feeling the carnal sensation overtaking me.

His hand moves between my legs and presses down, massaging wildly. My body ignites and bursts into heat and euphoric waves of blissful contractions that curl my toes. He's still behind me, and his cock remains lodged deep inside while my orgasm pulses against his member.

Sex with him isn't sex. It's like a drug that's worth more than all the chocolate in the world.

After a few long moments, my body floats back down to reality, and Dean pulls out.

"Not again," he grumbles.

Uh-oh. "The condom broke again?"

He moves off the bed and disappears into the bathroom. I turn and flop down on my back, spreading my arms. I'm spent. My muscles are Jell-O. I've never felt like such a happy, hopeful mess.

Turns out, I was right. It was no big deal making a plan for us. Dean moved in—*hottest roommate ever! So much naked time.* I'm staying put in my job for now, and Dean's going to finish his degree.

Between juggling our schedules, the nanny we found, and Coach and Jo, we have plenty of care for Fia. Even Flip has come over to sit for us once so we could have our first real date. Dean took me to the drive-in. I have no idea what movie was playing, but the sex was incredible.

After college, Dean already has contingent offers from two different NFL teams. One in Florida and one in Texas. Basically, they'll take him as long as he signs on within thirty days after his graduation and his stats remain the same. No, his current team didn't take home the big trophy this season, but they went to the playoffs and landed in the number two national slot. Dean handed them four out of five touchdowns. Not bad.

Of course, nothing is for sure, but it's what we've decided to do.

As a team.

It'll give me two more years of experience at the winery before Dean goes pro. The agreement is he'll play for three to five years. We'll use the money to buy a winery once we find something we like. When he retires, we'll build our little slice of wine heaven.

Turns out, the man has a knack for wine. Seriously. He can name a varietal with one whiff of the glass—his secret talent.

He truly is the perfect guy. At least for me.

Even his brother is a pretty perfect brother-in-law-to-be. Flip took Dean's old room at the man-cave, and I've never seen anyone more determined to turn his life around. He goes to meetings every day. He got a job. He's literally becoming a health-food freak and started writing a book about his crazy journey to sobriety. I know Dean is nervous about what the public will say, but he loves his brother more than he cares about his image.

As for our friend Tony, he didn't make it. The man apparently owed people money, which was the real reason he was after Marli. Life insurance. Tony had actually called in a tip to the police to ensure she was identified. That way he'd get the death certificate. Tony's downfall was his ego. If he hadn't called Dean, he might've gotten away with it. I'm glad he didn't. I never knew Marli, but she gave me the most incredible daughter. For that, I will always be grateful.

Oh, and yes. We finally learned the truth about Fia. She is Dean's. And now she's about to get a brother or sister. Dean doesn't know yet.

Dean emerges from the bathroom with a towel around his waist. He plops down on the edge of the bed. "I'm sorry, Lara. I think it's my curse. They just don't make condoms in my size."

He's actually sulking about having a big dick? Hilarious. I know women—and some men—who'd kill for a sex toy like that.

"Are you sure you don't want to go on birth control?" he asks. "Because I don't know what else to do."

After the last condom incident, we agreed I'd go

to the doctor and get a prescription. I kept my word, but it was two broken condoms too late. I told Dean a little white lie about the pill not being an option for me, but really, I've been waiting for the right moment to break the news. Definitely after his finals. And what better Christmas present. Right?

Unless he freaks the hell out? Then not a great present.

Either way, I know he'll be happy in the long run. This man was born for two things: to fight and to love.

"Dean? Christmas is still a few weeks away, but what if I give you your present early?"

"You just gave it to me." He leans down and kisses me between my naked breasts. "But I could always use another."

I smile. "I'm glad you said that, because another is exactly what you're getting."

Dean's eyes go wide, and his gaze locks on my face.

I nod. "That's right. Get ready because in eight months, you'll be catching something other than a football."

"Seriously?"

"Yep."

He stands and holds up two hands, index fingers pointed toward the sky. "Touchdown, baby! Yeah."

Not exactly the response I was looking for, but I'll take it.

DEAN

Plans be damned. I fucking love my life! I love this woman! I love this little baby! And I already love the one on the way.

I'm just a man, driving five hundred miles, enjoying every damned second.

THE END ←LOOK! NO CLIFFY!

Want more OHellNO? Check here for updates or sign up for new release alerts:
www.mimijean.net/ohellno
www.mimijean.net/get-news-from-mimi

AUTHOR'S NOTE

Hello, OHellNO fans!

I often think of my writing journey as a multi-layered cake. You just gotta have that rich dark-chocolate layer to fully appreciate the sweet creamy grenache. Rom-com is definitely what breaks up the heaviness and reminds me of all the beauty in life. Laughter is my fuel even if I'm writing about the dark side of life.

So I hope you enjoyed *BABY, PLEASE* as much as I did! Because what comes next is my first dive into horror-romance.

Let me be clear! It won't be gory. But if I do my job right, you will be sitting on the edge of your seat, praying for our H&H not to be gobbled up by monsters.

So get ready! **Mimi Monsters are coming!**

Be sure you're signed up for alerts of upcoming releases so you don't miss out: **www.mimijean.net/get-news-from-mimi**

And now onto your favorite part. FREE BOOK-MARKS!

STEP ONE: Email me at Mimi@mimijean.net

STEP TWO: Provide your complete shipping info (include the country if you're outside the US).

STEP THREE: If you wrote a review for *BABY, PLEASE* because you loved it and are one of those cool people who show support for your favorite authors, be sure to provide a link or screenshot. I will do my very best to include extra goodies. I run out of magnets fast! It's first ask, first get! But you will get a big THANK YOU from me either way.

STEP FOUR: Give me about 3–4 weeks. I'm pretty slow at getting snail mail out, but I do get to it. I send email confirmations once they go.

Thank you to all the OHellNO fans who keep me energized with their enthusiasm! I can't believe this is book #7 and that the series started in 2017. The series is going on six years!

WITH LOVE,
Mimi

PS – LISTEN TO MY PLAYLIST HERE
open.spotify.com/playlist/1mtv1xa5871NDUoRjBir
E9?si=0136d61be0a34c56

ACKNOWLEDGMENTS

Thank you, team Mimi! Book #55! As always, my appreciation goes out to all the awesome people who put their time into making my work shine and grammatically correct! Stephanie, LD, Paul, Pauline, Su, Kylie, Jaycee, and Joan.

Thank you to my dudes and family for not hating me when I talk about my characters at the dinner table.

With Love,
Mimi

Looking for another exciting read?
Check out *Mr. Ultra Mega Love*

CHAPTER ONE

JOY FERRIS

I'm curled into a tight ball on the locker room floor, begging for my life. The pain is too horrible to give a shit about which girl from the cheerleading squad is delivering the blows. Face, arms, back. Pain.

I'm in serious trouble here, and no one's coming to help. They made sure of that. The entire school, including my friends and teachers, are busy with finals, or they're out on the field, preparing for tomorrow's grad ceremony.

I yelp with the next blow, unable to stop myself from crying in front of them even though I don't want to. But what's the point in pretending they didn't just crack my rib or that my nose isn't broken? Or that, save a miracle, I am about to die? They aren't going to stop until *I* stop. Breathing.

My mind starts drifting in and out of con-sciousness, producing a string of random thoughts: *Who will protect my little brother? I never learned to dance salsa. I wish superheroes were real, and they'd come to save me.*

And just like that, I see my heroes surrounding me. Hope, Dreams, and the all-important Love. Funny how they look like versions of me in differ-ent-colored capes that match their hair. White, blue, and red. In real life, I'm a dirty blonde.

"Tsk-tsk," says Hope in white. "Such a shame that this is how it ends for you, Joy."

"Yeah," says Dreams, shaking her head of bright blue hair. "Just when I thought you'd made it, too. Valedictorian. Eighteen at last. Full scholarship."

"And you had such a bright future," says Love in red.

My mother said something similar last Sunday,

when we gathered for a little pre-graduation BBQ. Kyle and Huff, my two brothers—one older, one younger—chipped in with my parents to buy me a trip to Disney so I could go with my friends.

So sweet. So thoughtful. But that's the sort of thing my close-knit family does, because my success is their success. Their triumphs are my triumphs.

And now my death will be their pain.

"Maybe you should fight back," says Hope, arching a platinum-blonde brow, crossing her arms.

I want to fight, but it's no use. There're four of them and only one of me. They're ruthless. I'm not. I've never been able to inflict pain on anyone. Not intentionally. It's my Achilles' heel.

As the beating continues alongside my superhero hallucinations, a new wish sparks in my mind. I wish that, when people died, they could give their one best trait or skill to a person they love.

Wouldn't that be awesome?

You spend your entire life learning to paint like da Vinci, and on your death bed you get to pass along all your talent to one lucky person. Or maybe you're a gourmet chef. Maybe you've read five thousand books, and all that knowledge could be shared.

In my case, I would pass along my heart. I've always known it had too much love inside. More than my fair share. It's why I'm lying here on the floor, about to die and feeling so, so sorry for these girls. They just don't get it. They don't understand how their lives are about to change forever. No one kills an innocent human being and comes out the other side unchanged.

"Stop. Please stop," I whimper between the belts and kicks, but my pleas are no longer for me. They're for *them*. For these girls' souls. For my family when my bloodied body is found shoved into a locker or in a ditch somewhere.

Of course, no one will step forward to point a finger because their families run the town.

It's the reason my older brother, Kyle, is running for city councilman right out of college. The town's power families laughed him off until a poll showed he's about to get over seventy percent of the votes. People are sick and tired of letting a handful of fake do-gooders run this place like it's their personal kingdom. The challenge is long overdue.

I just didn't have the heart to tell Kyle about the repercussions of his choice—the threats, the elbows in the ribs between classes, and the gum magically appearing in my hair once a week. Not when he would drop out of the race because of it. Nothing matters more to him than family. He's one of those guys. Protective to the core.

Then there's Huff. Hudson Ulysses Ferris. Born six weeks early. Small for his age. Scared of his own shadow. He's the baby of our family, who lives trapped in a bubble of fear. I think it's because my parents always treated him like he's fragile. He's tougher than he knows, but in their minds, he never left that preemie chamber. It clouds everything they say or let him do, and he's been drinking their Kool-Aid. It's why he ran to my room after his first day of high school nine months ago, crying because he'd been dumped in a garbage can by some dickhead seniors. The next day, I gave those jerks a piece of my mind and went to the principal.

Detention.

Really?

That was it?

So typical of this damned town.

And even though I'm the one who told, Huff hasn't been able to shake the rep of tattletale pussy. He cries *almost* every night, wishing his rep weren't true. Sometimes, I cry for him. I'd give anything to make him see that his life could be happy. He's not worthless or weak. Fuck no. It's the bullies of this world who are tormented by insecurity, so they live life like hammers. *See a nail. Hit it.* Kill, end, destroy, cancel anyone who doesn't agree with them.

"Hey! Let up. I think Mrs. Mosley is coming," says one of the girls who's keeping watch by the locker room door.

Lana maybe? Perhaps it's Tasha. No, it has to be Manda. Her mom is the councilwoman about to lose her seat to Kyle.

A pair of lips graze my ear, speaking with the venomous hiss of a cobra. "You tell anyone about this, and I'll be sure your little brother gets ass-raped by the entire football team. Got it?"

I know the guys on the team. They wouldn't do that because they're a bunch of homophobes, but they'd sure as hell fuck up Huff if Manda snapped her perfectly manicured fingers.

"Tell me you understand, bitch," says…yes, it's Manda speaking now. I recognize the sugary stink of her perfume. "Say it."

I try to move my head and nod but can't. Too much pain.

"She's going to say something," warns one of the other girls. Tasha probably.

"I'm not missing graduation because of her white-trash ass," says another.

"Shut up. Just leave. I'll take care of this," replies Manda. "Joy isn't going to say a word."

No. Probably not. But my superheroes will.

I give my heart to you, Huff. I hope it gives you strength to dream and find yourself. I hope it helps you find love after I'm gone.

FIND OUT WHAT HAPPENS NEXT:
www.mimijean.net/ultramegalove

ABOUT THE AUTHOR

MIMI JEAN PAMFILOFF is a *New York Times* bestselling author who's sold over one million books around the world. Although she obtained her MBA and worked for more than fifteen years in the corporate world, she believes that it's never too late to come out of the romance closet and follow your dreams.

Mimi lives with her Latin lover hubby, two pirates-in-training (their boys), and their three spunky dragons (really, just very tiny dogs with big atti-tudes) Snowy, Mini, and Mack, in the vampire-unfriendly state of Arizona.

She hopes to make you laugh when you need it most and continues to pray daily that leather pants will make a big comeback for men.

Sign up for Mimi's mailing list for giveaways and new release news!

STALK MIMI:
www.mimijean.net
pinterest.com/mimijeanromance
instagram.com/mimijeanpamfiloff
facebook.com/MimiJeanPamfiloff

www.ingramcontent.com/pod-product-compliance
Lightning Source LLC
Chambersburg PA
CBHW071402150726
48000CB00001B/123